LINGER

A 7DS BOOKS COLLABORATION

7dsbooks.com

Linger

Published by

Twisted Core Press Short Story imprint 7DS Books

Smithfield, North Carolina, U.S.A.

This is a work of fiction. Any similarity with real persons or events is purely coincidental. Persons, events, and locations are either the product of the author's imagination, or used fictitiously.

Cover Image by

Cover design property of C. Anderson Picarella

CONTENTS

LADY ON FIRE

Kat Daughtry

The gnarled roads of the mountainside knotted Holly's stomach as she bumped against her sister's shoulder in the backseat of the family station wagon. Her stepfather seemed to enjoy fighting the curves beneath the canopy of pecan trees. The breeze knocked nuts onto the car roof in time with the music on the radio. The radio and the nuts left her head aching.

Elvis was playing on the radio. Elvis made everything better. He was a military man, like her father. Her real father. But he was still on a ship somewhere overseas. Elvis had come home months ago. If her dad was home, she didn't know it. She just knew he'd never find her. This was their third move since her dad left port.

Robert, stepfather extraordinaire, was a preacher, bouncing across the Carolinas from church to church, preaching the Word and pressing his wife's family into whatever housing the church could afford to offer. An endless cycle of hellfire and damnation.

"Here we are."

Robert slowed the wagon only enough to swerve onto the dirt path barely open between even more pecan trees. Holly smiled at her younger brother and sister. If they didn't seem happy, Robert would surely blame her.

As the car approached the house looming ahead, surrounded by weeping willows and overgrown grass, the radio crackled. Elvis's sweet tones faded as the dial bounced from side to side. Robert banged his hand against the dash. The dial stopped. A new song played through the static:

Scent of magnolias, sweet and fresh- Then the sudden smell of burning flesh.

"I never like that Elvis fool anyway," Robert shrugged.

The house was beautiful, and larger than Holly had expected. Her nerves calmed a bit. Robert had actually come through this time. This was not the normal ratty apartment or parsonage in despair. Two pick-up trucks waited for them next to their new parsonage.

Robert shut the engine off and looked at Holly. "Do not embarrass me, child."

Holly looked at her mother for support, but all she received was a half-smile from the corner of her mother's lips. Holly nodded and nudged her siblings to exit the stuffy heat of the wagon. The young ones scooted out the bench seat and followed behind her. Holly waited behind her mother as Robert greeted the two men in conversation between the trucks.

"Preacher Rob, nice to meet you." A short lanky older gentleman greeted him with a handshake.

Holly watched as the lanky man walked her stepfather around the outside of the property. The other man, a round fellow, remained against his truck and offered them a nod. Her mother waited for Robert without a step toward the home.

"I can handle anything, sir." Robert was boasting about

himself as he returned with the lanky man. He continued on about his dedication to God and the Good Word, as well as his strength built as retired sailor. The lanky man nodded along but Holly could tell that Robert's self-proclaimed greatness was already annoying the man. She smiled. She may very well like this little pecan covered town after all.

"This is Sheriff Lawrence Narron." The lanky man offered Robert a proper introduction to the round man.

"Sheriff?" Robert laughed. "Expecting trouble with the new preacher?"

"I always meet new residents," the large uniformed man explained. "Especially the one's living in the parsonage."

"Will I see you in church, then?" Robert winked and nudged.

"You'll see lots of me, Preacher Rob. I am sure of it."

"Good to hear. Good to hear." Robert stuck his hands inside his pants pockets and tilted heel to toe as he waited to see the inside of the house.

The Sheriff looked toward Holly and her family, tipping his hat at her mother. "Gotta run. I'll see y'all soon."

"Stop by for dinner sometime this week, Sheriff," her mother offered.

He climbed into his truck and closed the door without a word. His tires rolled softly as he passed their family, then a dirt cloud polluted the path behind him once he edged far enough away to bolt down the path. He vanished behind the pecan trees. Robert and the lanky fellow walked onto the large covered porch.

"Come along," Robert called, then turned back to the man beside him. "This is Vivian, my wife, and her kids," he introduced them without looking back.

"*Her* kids, you say?" his brows arched.

"I do what I can," Robert replied piously.

The lanky man turned and bowed toward Vivian. "I'm Deacon Norris."

The deacon led the family inside. The smell of newness hit them in the face. Holly expected old, worn and worthy of free with the job of preacher sort of home, but Holly could hardly believe her eyes. Her mother gasped at the sights of the interior.

"As I said over the phone, just like new, down to the furniture." The deacon stood aside for the family to explore.

"I must admit, I had wondered if you could have been so sincere with those words," Robert rubbed his finger across an entry table as if he were conducting a white glove inspection, "This is nice."

"Yes sir." Deacon Norris nodded.

"I don't know what to say." Vivian laughed.

"Nothing to clean, Vivian." Robert patted her bottom.

"Telephone and lights are on already," the Deacon added, "well water, of course."

"So, the church pays for everything?" Vivian held her chest.

"Not everything." Deacon Norris shook his head.

"Deacon has me a job lined up as butcher at the market. That will pay for food as well as odds and ends."

Holly relaxed at the thought of Robert working away from home. Her mother was different when he wasn't around. They all were. It was calm when he went away. *He would enjoy hacking away at meat all day,* she giggled to herself.

Holly's mother took the children for a tour of the house while the men discussed the details of the arrangements. The upstairs bedroom Holly would share with her sister was large. It only had one window but it was the length of one wall and close to the height. Holly gazed out the window while Ellen bounced on both of the beds. Holly spied the largest willow tree she had ever seen. It swept over a pond she couldn't see from the front of the house. The dangling branches danced on top of the water.

"May I take the kids to swim, mother?" Holly pleaded.

"Not now," her mother answered. "First we need to unload the car so Robert can drive into town."

"Unpack the car and then we can swim?" Holly countered.

Her mother sighed. "Fine." Then she backed out of the way as the kids rushed past her.

~*~

It didn't take long for the three kids to unpack the station wagon. Her mother remained inside unpacking items as they were brought to her. Robert handled his own things to make sure the kids didn't ruin anything important. Holly lugged in the final box and placed it on the polished kitchen table. She waited for her mother's permission to change into swim clothes.

With a simple nod, her mother winked and the kids raced into their rooms. Holly was the first one changed and waited for the younger ones by the side of the pond. The heat of the day crowned her head with beads of sweat. Paul darted across the thick grass and jumped into the water without saying a word or contemplating waiting, but Ellen only slowly made her own way toward the pond. Step by slow step. Once she was close to the pond, that was good enough for Holly to leap into the water.

Nothing compared to that first jump after waiting so long. Holly remained underwater to let the coolness blanket her from the heat above. She could feel the fish tickling her legs as she swam deeper, but soon enough time had passed for her to need a moment above for air. She pushed her toes into the shallow bottom near the edge and pushed off.

Panic set in. Something wrapped around her ankle. She used her free foot to try to push off whatever had grasped her. Nothing worked. It had her tightly and she could feel the pressure of her skin threatening to rip the more she tried to break free.

She could hear herself screaming, *Help me!* in her mind.

The lack of air ballooned inside her chest like a fireball. She had to breathe, even if she only had water to fill her lungs. Her mouth opened and just as instantly as her foot was caught, it was released. Choking on water, she splashed to the top for air.

She collapsed in the grass as tears flooded her eyes. She could barely hear Ellen and Paul shrill with worry as she coughed the water from her lungs. Her mother rushed to her, beating the water and air out by slapping her back. She finally caught her breath and fell onto her side, tears running down her face.

"What happened?" Her mother scooped her head into her lap.

"I cried for help and no one heard me."

"You cried for help underwater and no one heard you?" Robert taunted as he walked to her side. "That doesn't even make a bit of logical sense, Holly."

She paused. "I know."

~*~

Dinner went by with little conversation. Vivian and Robert discussed the possibility of the willow's roots edging into the sides of the pond. It was quite possible for that to be the cause of Holly's mishap. Robert ended the conversation once Vivian suggested cutting the roots away. He didn't like to mess with nature. He demanded the kids simply use common sense.

Vivian didn't push him. She rubbed the top of Holly's hand and passed the conversation along to rambles of meeting locals before church and ways to do so. The children finished dinner and cleared their spots before settling into their new rooms for the night. Holly tucked Paul into his bed and read Ellen a story before crawling into her own foreign resting spot.

She watched the moonlight dance across the pond. The shadows of the willow tree grew eerie with the night. The crickets carried on their melody until she fell asleep with the summer's natural lullaby. It had been too long since she recalled the sounds of a country night. Robert had a fondness of the city.

She tossed and turned, working a sweat in the still of the humid night. She flipped her pillow over and over until no coolness existed within the fluff. Her dreams haunted her with the water. She heard her cries for help. The cries no one could hear. They echoed inside her mind until her voice no longer sounded like her own.

Her eyes popped open as she gasped for air. She moved her feet only to make sure the dream was over. They rubbed freely against the sheet. Her heart steadied as her breath caught inside her chest. Her head rolled to the side enough to assure herself that she had not startled Ellen.

The silence pierced the night. The crickets' lullaby had ended yet the sun didn't come close to cutting through the night sky. Quietly, she rolled from the bed and made her way toward the enormous window to let in some air. It was hard to figure out, half asleep and with only the light of the moon. Parts of the window opened, allowing some breeze into the thickness of the room.

Just as Holly turned back to her bed, something caught her eye: a flicker of orange beside the willow. She rubbed her eyes to only see the same moonlight dance against the water. Her feet dragged the floor until she fell back into the comfort of her bed and slept soundly through the night.

~*~

The next few days passed with ease. Robert started his job as a butcher immediately and spent his evenings working on a *"true plan"* for his new church. Vivian used moments when Robert was not using the family station wagon to venture into town and introduce herself and invite people to the church. Holly spent her time looking after her siblings. Most days were spent carefully swimming in their private pond.

The first Sunday at their new church had finally arrived. Holly and her siblings were used to new churches. Robert always said he floated wherever the Lord needed him. Holly was rather certain the churches of their past had only grown tired of Robert as a self-proclaimed saint. Vivian hustled around the house, in a panic, trying to make sure their first day was nothing less than true Southern perfection.

They strolled down the dirt path toward the pecan trees, fully dressed in the top of their Sunday's best, and loaded into the station wagon. The car was silent. The radio stopped working the day after their arrival. Robert desperately wanted to blame the kids. He wanted to blame Holly. But Vivian stood firm on the fact that the kids had not been near the car since they unloaded it.

Holly hated not having the radio. Not only did that mean no chance of hearing Elvis, it also gave Robert the need to consume the silence after a bit. Once he started, he didn't stop. He told the same stories all the time. He never kept the facts straight, though.

The kids had listened to no less than a hundred stories of how he met their father. Each one consisted of Robert somehow saving the day or teaching their father a common sense lesson. Holly learned to tune him out and play Elvis songs inside her mind. Vivian laughed along with each story and would politely say, "Oh, I never knew that!" It made Holly sick.

The church was decent in size. Cars flooded around the building. It was an established church. Old, by the looks of it as well as by the size of the cemetery span. Holly enjoyed the graves connected to the churches. She liked to visit them, take the name, do the math to figure the age of the deceased, and create the story of how they might have died.

She tip-toed away from her family and barely made it to the gate entrance of the cemetery before her mother noticed and called for her to join them. *Later,* she thought. The church family seemed as welcoming as any other church they had passed through. The older members embraced with hugs and smiles. The children whispered and pretended to be sociable when parents were watching.

They took their seats on the front row pew. The deacon's wife and child joined them. Robert spent most of the time telling his story. His testimony. He mentioned Vivian once and the children, not at all. A few hymns filled the chapters of his heroic and ever so Godly life and the service was over.

Vivian always invited the members of a church over to the home for dinner after service. But this time, everyone seemed to have plans. Holly wondered how quickly the new congregation must have figured her stepfather out considering no one jumped on the chance for a free dinner.

"Rather odd nobody wanted to visit the new preacher," Vivian broke the silence on the way home from church.

"Shut up," Robert snapped.

"Nothing against you," she apologized with a rub against his leg.

"I know."

"Maybe I pushed a bit much," she searched for an excuse.

"Probably."

~*~

After a dinner of Robert blaming Vivian and Holly and the deacon and everyone else for no one coming to dinner, Vivian rushed Holly out of the room to wash her siblings before bed. She had no problem listening and vanishing from Robert's sight before he could respond. She sang as the water ran. She did everything in her power to keep the younger ones from hearing that man yell at their mother. She knew they could still hear, but she retained most of their attention.

They had all settled into bed before their mother made her way through the darkness for prayers and nightly kisses. Her mother seemed so beautiful against the moonlight. She kissed Holly last and said her prayers along with her.

She leaned over to kiss Holly against the cheek once more before leaving the room. Holly knew her mother loved her. She wouldn't stay near danger for her kids, not even for Robert. She was almost positive. She watched as the door shut, leaving only the flickering moonlight outside the already opened window.

Holly woke in the middle of the night. Not a single bad dream or memory had haunted her. Her eyes popped open and she was fully awake. She tossed and turned until sitting up seemed to be the only option. She watched the willow branches flow with the breeze from the window.

It was only when she noticed the silence that the crickets began to sing again. It didn't settle well with her. She walked her way across the room and stopped as the crickets silenced, again. She walked back toward the window. She was certain a faint glow glistened below the pond water. The mysterious light vanished as the crickets sounded again.

She tip-toed across the room and into her bed. Her skin felt cool. Too cool for a hot summer's night. She nestled into the warmth of her bedding. The chill remained no matter how tightly she tucked herself into the covers.

Her eyes had barely closed from exhaustion when she heard the screams. A woman ran beneath her window, screaming for help. Holly ran to the window, heart racing. She saw no one. The cries seemed further away. She ran toward her door to get her mother and Robert but as her hand grabbed the knob, the voice screamed right by her window.

She ran back toward the window and called to the frightened woman. There was no reply. Her mother ran into the room and switched the light on. Robert yelled from the hall to cut the light off. Vivian obeyed.

"What did you see, Holly?"

"I saw nothing, Mama. No one."

"I'll stay here near you girls and Paul. Robert will handle it."

Holly frowned. "Oh, now I feel safe."

Her mother arched her brow as she opened the doors of the joining bathroom to keep an eye over both rooms. Ellen and Paul remained asleep during the cries, even as they sounded every few moments. Robert ran around outside with a light and a gun trying to find the poor woman. Her cries turned into blood curdling screams as her voice circled the property.

Robert couldn't keep up with her. His calls to her seemed to be too far beyond her voice. Eventually, Holly heard something splash into the pond and silence fell over the night. The crickets returned moments later. Robert staggered, exhausted, back inside and secured every lock on the door.

"What should we do?" Vivian whispered.

"I'll call the Sheriff. Stay with your kids."

Vivian curled into the bed beside Holly. Their hearts raced together. There was no comfort. Robert finally returned and called Vivian into the hallway. Holly listened.

"The son of a bitch isn't coming out," Robert huffed.

"How could he not?"

"The bastard says this mess happens all the time. Teenagers fooling most likely. Nothing to do, especially now that it seems to be over."

"Keeping the haunting alive," Vivian nodded.

"So you heard about that, huh?"

"Did you think I wouldn't? Small mountain town with nothing but gossip for entertainment?"

"So, I guess next time, I'll just shoot the stupid ass kids and be done with the nonsense."

"Robert, seriously." She closed the door to the bedroom. Holly had heard enough to ease her mind, but somehow it didn't.

~*~

Her restless eyes struggled through the day. Holly and Vivian didn't dare mention a word of the night before around the younger ones. They didn't play outside that day. The mother convinced the children it was simply too hot of a day. Holly backed her up fully and occupied the kids inside.

Robert came home from a day of butchering just as exhausted as Holly and Vivian. A peaceful dinner followed long bouts of silence. Vivian bathed the younger children along with Holly. She wanted to stay near the children. Robert cleaned his gun and prepared for the possibility of another sleepless night.

Prayers and kisses were passed out and Vivian left the kids to sleep. Both doors to the joining bathroom were left open as well as both bedroom doors. Robert and Vivian chatted quietly in the front room with the lights off as they waited for the hooligans to return to scare them. Holly remained awake well past the snores of Robert and the silence of her mother in the front room. She listened to the crickets. She listened to the silence following.

Her stomach knotted. She knew what was to come. Her knuckles blanched as she gripped the edges of the white cotton sheets. She could see the light out the window grow brighter than the faintness of the moon. She waited but nothing happened.

Her knobby knees hit the hardwood floor with a thud as she attempted to roll from her bed. She crawled at a snail's pace across the room. Her hands and knees creaked against the floor. Her heart raced as she nestled directly below the window. She swallowed the lump in her throat and took a deep breath. Her eyes edged toward the window sill. The breath from her nose fogged the window. She tried not to breathe.

The pond carried a haunting glow brighter than before. It flickered like flames beneath the surface. Holly watched until the light faded back into darkness. The crickets stayed mute.

The tension remained, but she felt foolish kneeling by the window with nothing to see. She rose to her feet, facing the door to make sure her mother did not see her out of bed. She turned back, to give a final glance outside.

Holly screamed as her eyes locked directly into the face of a phantom. A ring of fire wrapped the rim of each haunting eye outside the window. The flesh was nothing more than a charred and blackened casing, shadowing only the whites of the fiery eyes and a mouth without lips. Holly fell onto her bed before her scream ceased. Ellen jumped from hers.

Robert and her mother ran into the room flicking the light switch. Robert held his gun, ready to fire. Vivian grabbed her daughter and wrapped her arms around her, begging for information.

"A burnt lady!" Holly screamed. "Dead. Out my window!"

Robert flicked the light off again. He raced to the window and scoped as far as his eyes would view. His gun pointed along with his sight. He waited for a sign to shoot. Nothing happened. He growled and lowered his gun.

"Damn foolery." He shook the gun toward the young girl. "You'll not make a fool of me, Holly!"

He placed his gun along the deepness of the window sill and reached to undo his belt for a lashing. Before his buckle disconnected, the shrills began. The screaming woman had returned. Ellen began to cry. Robert grabbed his gun, instructed Vivian to call the Sheriff, and stomped out the front door.

Holly held onto Ellen. Paul ran to her, crying as well. She cradled them both as her mother called for the Sheriff. They watched in the darkness as Robert ran circles around the house. He fell further behind the burnt woman with each run around the property.

Holly listened to her mother's conversation with the Sheriff. *"I promise you, you will get your lard ass out of bed and come down here....Yes, I am the preacher's wife...Don't tell me what sort of language to use. I have three children here, scared to damn death..... Come do your job....Oh yeah, well, fuck you, you fat ass son of a devil's whore. How's that for religious?"* She slammed the phone.

Eventually, the young ones fell asleep. Robert returned inside. Vivian apologized for her language. He laughed. The three of them had another sleepless night.

~*~

The next few nights repeated the same events. The entire household fell ill with exhaustion. They listened to the screams at night and altered their schedule to sleeping with the sunshine. Robert slept in the early evenings after work. He stopped chasing the woman.

Her screams lasted longer and longer each night. Robert's temper grew with each unsettling night. Holly wanted her father. Her real father. She wondered each night if he could feel her suffering. She made the mistake of mentioning aloud her desperation in missing her father just as the nightly screams had just ended. Robert snapped.

He pulled his belt off and cracked it between his hands as a warning of what Holly was about to receive. Vivian stood between them, covering Holly with her own body. He threw his wife to the side, knocking her onto a side table and busting it. Ellen and Paul screamed for him to leave her alone. He didn't listen.

He drew the belt over his head and flexed his muscle to lash her with full force. Holly cowered beside the wooden radio. Her arms covered her face and she screamed, waiting for his punishment. Before he could swing a stroke of the belt, the wooden radio screeched with static and blared the last song the car radio played.

> *Scent of magnolias, sweet and fresh- Then the sudden smell of burning flesh.*

Robert stood frozen over her. She lowered her arms. A blanket of safety washed over her. The song gave her goose bumps, but she knew she was safe, at least from Robert. He dropped the belt and stomped to his room, slamming the door behind him.

Vivian gathered the children and led them into the girls' room, door locked behind them. Holly crawled into bed with Ellen and gave her bed to her mother and Paul. Long moments of silence fell into short moments of rest until the sun rose again. Vivian waited until she heard Robert drive away for work before getting out of bed. Holly followed her into the kitchen.

"Will you feel safe here alone with the children?"

"During the day, yes." Holly rested her head against the kitchen table.

"Days are quiet." Vivian sighed.

"I'm not really afraid of the nights anymore. I just wish I could help her."

"You don't think it's a teenager fooling around?"

"Mother, I saw her. Burnt to a crisp. Fire in her eyes."

"You were tired."

"She cries for help and nobody saves her."

"And you know how that feels." Tears swelled the bottom of Vivian's eyes.

Holly said nothing. Her mother kissed her brow and walked out of the room to make a phone call. After asking someone for a ride to town, she vanished into her room and returned moments later, fully dressed. Holly prepared breakfast for Ellen and Paul. They both sat silently and watched the young ones eat.

It wasn't long before a car horn honked from outside. Vivian kissed her children goodbye and dashed out the door. Holly followed to the window to see her mother leaving with the deacon's wife. She thought she would never see that car in the yard again. She smiled.

The day passed slowly as she waited for her mother to return. Afternoon neared evening and Holly feared Robert would return before her mother. She cooked a solid meal to occupy him just in case he did make it home first. She fed the kids early, bathed them and let them play in their rooms. She heard tires rolling against the pebbled dirt of the driveway.

Holly peered from the curtain to not be seen. It was her mother. The deacon's wife even shut the car off and helped her mother unload bags of groceries. It was not possible for her mother to be gone all day for a simple grocery run. She opened the door and held it as they entered.

"Hello, sweetie," the deacon's wife greeted her.

"Hello." Holly stood puzzled.

Robert pulled into the drive just as Vivian made her way into the house with her arms full of paper bagged groceries. Holly's stomach sank at the sight of him. She officially hated him and wished he would die. Maybe if he would die, her daddy could return to her mother and they would all be safe. She swallowed her animosity and held the door for him as well.

"Mrs. Norris," Robert nodded, "I didn't think I'd see you except on Sundays."

"Well, your lovely wife gave me a wake up call today," she

giggled.

"Wake up call?"

"Yes. In fact, she gave half of the town a wake up call today. We've all been mighty horrible examples of Christians." The Deacon's wife shot him a knowing glance. "We all do that from time to time."

"Yes," he agreed.

Vivian and Holly unloaded the groceries and put them away. Anne continued to explain to Robert what Vivian had accomplished around town today. She informed him that the Sheriff was on his way over to discuss the events of the sleepless nights. He could explain it better than anyone, she said. Robert nodded along, still unsure of the sudden support his wife had managed to muster.

Headlights flashed through the window of the front room. "Let the sheriff in, Holly," Robert called.

Holly held the door open for the large man. He didn't speak to her. His face carried concern and an agitated expression. He strolled past her and claimed a spot at the kitchen table beside Robert, Anne, and her mother. Holly listened from the hallway.

"I have never been talked to by anyone in this damn town the way your wife has talked to me twice now, Robert." The Sheriff placed his hat on the table top.

"I apologize, sir." Robert glared at his wife.

"Don't. I deserved it. We all did. We keep doing good folk horrible. But we ain't bad. We just don't know what the hell to do."

"Catch these people," Robert snapped. "That's what the hell you do. It's your job."

"It ain't even people, Robert." The Sheriff propped his face against his propped arm. "I'm sure they used to be. Pretty sure I know who they were."

"You're here giving me bullshit about ghosts, Sheriff?"

"I promise you, preacher, I don't bullshit."

Vivian placed a cup of coffee in front of each guest, as well as Robert. She carried a calm smile across her face. Holly was happy to see that return. She listened as her mother settled into the conversation.

"We are having a cookout." She smiled and waited.

"A damn cookout. We got ghosts and your fucking wife wants a cookout." The Sheriff plopped his hat back onto his head.

"What is a cookout supposed to do?" Anne questioned politely.

"I hear this ends on Independence Day." Vivian sipped her coffee. "So, we always have a cookout anyway. And when nothing happens because the little assholes behind this are too chicken-shit to carry on this little small mountain legend, it's done. Over. For all to see."

"Ma'am, not to be harsh," the sheriff replied, "but I've seen this. We ain't talking teenage bullshit. We are talking drop to your knees and pray to God, demonic fucking hell on earth. Pardon my language."

"So you all--the entire town--knows this happens. Why do you keep putting families in this house?" Vivian snarled.

"Honest, ma'am," the sheriff replied. "We just thought a good pure man of God could pray this shit away or something. Bless it. Damn it. Burn it... Something."

"So why not be honest?" Robert slammed his hands on the table.

"Would you be here if we were?" Anne laughed.

"Fix it, Robert," the sheriff begged. "Everyone else runs off."

"I'm not sure I know how."

"Either way. Ghost, demons, teenagers. Sunday, after church we will cookout, celebrate the holiday, and have the whole damned town here with us." Vivian dabbed her bright red lipstick against her coffee napkin.

"Church and a demonic cookout. I'm tickled damn pink we found you." The sheriff stood from the table and pushed his chair in. "I gotta get back to work."

"See you Sunday, Sheriff." Vivian winked.

"Walk me to my car and follow me out." Anne barked at the Sheriff as she stood.

"Glad to see you guys. Can't wait for Sunday." Robert didn't move from his spot.

The guests left and their car lights vanished into the darkness. Vivian fixed herself and Robert each a plate of food Holly had prepared. Holly gently eased her way into the kitchen. Robert kicked a chair out for her to sit down beside him.

"Your mother is nuts, Holly. Did ya know that?" He took a bite of food. "A fucking cookout."

"This isn't demons. It isn't ghosts. I half way wonder if it isn't the deacon and his fucked up little family."

"Now, why the holy hell would they do it?"

"Come on. Anne is the definition of false pleasantry. Such an ass kiss. Her husband has been deacon now through how many preachers? Yet, the church keeps pulling in new ones, overlooking him. That must hurt. You know he has all the education to be a preacher. Just like you. And the others."

"He doesn't want it. I asked him. I honestly felt like I

might be stepping on toes."

"Maybe he just doesn't want the house." Holly interrupted.

"Honey, taking the job doesn't mean they would have to take the house. He just wouldn't get paid in any form." She rubbed Holly's arm.

"I don't know, Mama." Holly crossed her arms. "I don't think it's people."

"Honey, ghosts are not real. And my goodness, if you could have seen the way Anne pushed me towards people that fully backed her jive of a story."

"Shouldn't that secure it as maybe true?" Holly questioned.

"The one thing I know about folklore *and* gossip...everyone has a different story. This feels fake."

"Well, here's to another sleepless night." Robert chugged his coffee and slammed the cup against the table.

~*~

By Sunday, her mother seemed was certain of two things. The deacon's family was behind the screaming lady and a cookout of Independence Day without the screaming lady would allow the town to feel safe visiting the parsonage again. Holly was not convinced. She hummed Elvis beneath her breath during the sermon. She felt the eyes burning into the back of her head during service. Nobody wanted to come to her house. Nobody.

Robert finished the service with a solid reminder of the cookout following church at his house. The family drove home in silence. When the canopy of pecan trees opened up into grass and willows, the broken radio turned into crackling static. The dial ran back and forth until the song played through heavy static.

Scent of magnolias, sweet and fresh- Then the sudden smell of burning flesh.

Robert tried to change the dial. It didn't work. The song remained. The volume didn't work. Everyone, tensed, listened in silence until Robert cut the car off in front of the house.

"That song is unsettling, I suppose." Vivian finally muttered with a crack in her voice.

"Everyone will be here soon. Let's hurry up." Robert ordered.

They all worked to set chairs up outside. Robert had already dug a hole off to the side for a fire pit. Vivian had prepared lots of food. The kids set it all out inside on the kitchen counter. Cars began to enter the yard.

It was by no means the entire church, much less the town. A few families braved the fear of Independence Day at the parsonage. Nobody spoke of it. The men talked politics and faith while the women discussed cooking and husbands. The kids barely played through fear of folklore.

Robert and another man carried the radio onto the front porch. The music helped. The radio played lots of Elvis and Holly was satisfied. Robert didn't trash talk Elvis in front of normal people. It was a real party.

The fire pit added spark to the gathering. The scent of food cooking on open flames lifted the all American spirits. The deacon and his family arrived as darkness set in. The sheriff followed shortly after. He had a wife and children. Holly was surprised to see such a brash man with an actual family.

Robert greeted him by his truck. "Hello, Sheriff."

"You got a water hose here?"

"Of course," Robert chuckled. "Afraid of the fire pit?"

"Not in the least, son," he spat and walked past him to greet other locals.

Robert connected the water hose in case he was facing some sort of burning penalty by not having it near the pit already. Vivian and the children greeted the sheriff's family. His wife seemed nervous, but his children were older. They seemed excited by the thoughts of what they called the *"Lady on Fire."*

"You'll see," they kept saying. "We'll all see. Finally."

Holly waited. The night grew long for her. Others seemed to have forgotten the purpose of the night. The men ate well beyond their limits. The women gossiped. The children played with sparklers. Holly walked alone toward the willow by the pond. The Sheriff yelled at her and suggested against it. She wasn't afraid of this *Woman on Fire*. She seemed like the only one she could relate to anymore. She wanted to meet her. Maybe she could help her.

Several people left the cookout early. Fear sets in well when even the moon decides to hide. It was dark beyond the light of the porch and a few random sparklers. The sheriff's teenage son walked over toward Holly. She could sense his fear. He tried to hide it as he sat beneath the willow beside her.

"It will glow," she whispered.

"The pond?" He nodded. "I've heard that."

"I've seen it."

"You aren't scared. I'm surprised."

"She won't hurt anyone. She just wants help."

"How do you help the dead?" he laughed.

"I don't even know how to help the living," she shrugged.

The sparkling light beneath the pond's surface flickered brightly beneath them. He tugged her arm, but she was captivated. Lost within the grasp of the light, she didn't hear Robert calling for her. She heard nothing. Silence.

The orange light of the pond grew stronger until her own eyes reflected with a ring of fire. Robert pulled her arm. She didn't move. He slapped her across the face. Vivian screamed from across the yard. He yanked her again, pulling her from the pond's edge.

Suddenly, the radio blared a crackling static. The visitors covered their ears. Captivated by the light, Holly dragged along behind Robert like a rag doll. The radio static stopped. The song played.

Scent of magnolias, sweet and fresh- Then the sudden smell of burning flesh.

Robert lost it. He threw Holly against the ground and kicked her gut before realizing his guests were watching. He wiped his nose and held his head lowly.

"I'm sorry. She doesn't think. I was scared."

"Oh, preacher." The sheriff backed away from him.

Robert jumped onto the porch. He kicked the stereo as he screamed about hating that song. He tried to change the dial. Nothing. He reached inside to unplug it. Cord in hand, the song played on. His face grew pale.

The guests watched in fear. The screaming began. It filled the air and didn't stop. Families bound tightly together. The deacon stood with arms tightly around son and wife. Vivian led Ellen and Paul into the hold of the sheriff's family, then ran toward Holly's motionless body.

The screams echoed through the willows. Vivian stopped short of reaching her daughter. An orange manifestation grew from the ground before Holly. Slowly it formed into the Lady on Fire. She stood between Vivian and her daughter, beautiful and engulfed in flames.

Holly held her hand toward the flaming lady. The flamed hand of the spirit met hers. Vivian yelled for her daughter.

"Holy hell. I've never seen her before!" the Sheriff called, locked around his loved ones as well as Holly's siblings. "Get the hose, Robert!"

"Fuck the hose!" Robert ran inside.

Ignoring the others, Holly and the Lady of Fire whispered to one another. "Help me."

The spirit smiled. She was dark skinned, with deep brown eyes inside the flame. Her belly curved round with child.

Holly smiled back. "Show me," she whispered.

The spirit nodded. Figures of flame flickered across the yard. Voices filled the air, audible above the endless screaming.

Why, David? We could vanish. Leave this town. Why are you doing this? This is our baby. You love me. Don't say you don't love me. You'll love this baby. Stop, David. You're hurting me! I don't want to get in the car!

"'David'," the Sheriff growled. "David fucking Norris."

"David Norris?" his wife squawked. "The deacon's father? He ran away with his sister's maid, that cute colored girl."

"Apparently not." The Sheriff shook his head. "Son of a bitch."

The flaming spirit shot her attention toward the Sheriff. She smiled. *Thank you,* she mouthed. He stood silently, shocked. The voices carried on near the glowing pond.

David, it hurts! Stop it, David! No! No!

Flames flickered near the drive way. Screams radiated from the flames. The Sheriff grabbed the hose as Robert ran through the door with a shotgun.

"What in the hell are you going to do with that?" the Sheriff laughed.

"Kill these sons of bitches."

Robert shot at the flames. The flames only raced across the yard, circling the house in the same course the screams had run each night before, scorching a ring around the property.

David, it hurts! Why, David? I love you! Why?

The women cried, listening to how this Lady on Fire met her tragic death. David Norris had burned her to death. Slowly. Painfully. The baby inside burning as well. His baby.

I need the pond! Let me get to the pond! It hurts! Dear God, put me out David! It hurts! Not the car! Don't put me in the car! David!

Holly looked at the flaming spirit beside her. She watched her lovely face melt and drip onto the ground. Her flesh withered and charred until she became the ghastly image she saw from her window. Only her teeth and the white in her eyes remained intact. Her eyes showed sorrow beyond the flames.

"You!" Robert shot at the spirit, the buckshot sailing harmlessly through the flaming apparition.

She turned to him. He shot again. She looked toward Holly. Robert did too, growling wide-eyed. He aimed his gun against the side of Holly's face. She closed her young eyes and begged the spirit.

"Help me."

The Lady on Fire engulfed Robert. He screamed. He ran for the pond. She didn't let go, her flames enrapturing him. He splashed into the pond, screaming. He cried. He begged for help. Nobody seemed to hear him.

"Spray the flames," the Sheriff ordered his son. "I'll call for help."

The Lady released Robert into the pond. He pulled himself ashore again and tossed around the grass beneath the willow tree.

The spirit returned to Holly. *You're safe,* Holly heard her voice in her mind. The middle of the pond splashed. The screams of the Lady on Fire echoed along, joined by the screams of Robert--and another man. But no one could find the owner of the other scream.

The deacon sobbed. "My father! That's my father's voice. I thought I hated the son of a bitch for running off with her. He killed her. Dammit! He killed her."

Drain it. Bury me. Away from him. The flaming spirit pointed toward the pond.

"I will." Holly wiped the tears from her eyes.

The spirit looked toward the porch. The radio returned to static before replacing the sad song of the lady on fire with Elvis. Holly smiled. The spirit silenced the screams. She floated toward the pond and vanished, taking the flickering light beneath the water with her.

Robert continued to scream and roll around the ground beneath the willow tree. The Sheriff's son cut the hose off just as the ambulance reached the drive way. The small crowd stood silent, in shock as the Sheriff explained to the paramedics how the preacher was obviously suffering from a severe mental breakdown. Holly watched as they bound his hands and carried him away.

Vivian wrapped her arms around her daughter. Holly smiled at the Sheriff as he stood before her. They stood within the spirits running ring of fire. Scorched footprints in the grass surrounded them in a perfect circle.

"Drain it." Holly demanded.

"Yes, young lady." He wiped sweat from his face. "First thing in the morning."

"No. She deserves it now."

"You heard her, you son of a devil's whore." Vivian smiled.

"You don't fuck with a preacher's wife. I got it. Let me call it in."

The deacon made his way across the yard. His head held in shame. "My father," he paused. "My God, my father. The almighty perfect preacher known for skipping out on me and mom. A murderer."

"I'm sorry, Deacon." Vivian offered a rub against his shoulder.

"May I watch?" he fairly begged. "May I see them drain this thing?"

"I'd rather not be alone with the kids tonight. I'd love for you all to stay the night. Please." Vivian offered.

Holly wandered away. She climbed into the moss covered willow tree by the pond. She refused sleep. Deacon and her mother brought her drink and checked on her. She remained solid against the heavy branches of the tree until the pond ran empty.

Finally, uncovered, the car. The deacon jumped in beside the crew. The family car of Old Preacher Norris. The car that trapped the Lady on Fire. Her remains were still there, right inside the car door that caught the preacher's tie as he gave the car a final push into the water.

TORMENTED

Dawn Kirby

"This is what we've been reduced to?" the voice in the shadows asked. "Surviving off the blood of the less fortunate? The innocent?"

He drifted into the soft glow of the candlelight, barely a mist of the noble man they'd once been. The vampire rolled his eyes at the ghost and melted into the mattress beside the dead woman. Tears filled the ghost's pale eyes as he brushed his transparent fingers across her cheek.

"Did you even consider what her death would do to her family?"

"Rest assured," Nathan said coolly, "she was alone." He tossed the sheet over her lifeless body and rolled off the bed. He put on his trousers then poured himself a glass of wine. "I'd offer you a glass," he chuckled, "but it would only go right through you. Such a waste."

"For that, I have only you to thank."

"I'm not the monster you make me out to be," Nathan complained.

"No, we are worse," he spat back. "You allowed that

creature to turn us knowing what her curse meant."

"I allowed it knowing it meant I would live forever. Had I known I would be saddled with your constant presence I may have had second thoughts." Nathan drank the wine and pitched the glass into the fireplace. "Contrary to what you may believe, morality no longer has a place in my life."

"Does it not? Are we not just as responsible for our actions as we were before? Do certain ramifications not follow the decisions you make on our behalf?"

"No. The decisions I make for me are purely beneficial."

"And what of the victims? Are their lives and that of those who loved them not also a concern? I can assure you, they find no benefit in loss."

"No benefit?" Nathan smiled wickedly and gestured toward the bed. "The way I see it I am performing a public service. I rid the streets of those who have been forgotten. I offer them warmth, food. I let them use my bath."

"All self-serving."

"So you say," Nathan grumbled. "The fact is nobody cares what happens to them. They are on the streets because they are unwanted, unloved. I give them what they need. What they long for. Then I release them from their misery."

The ghost glided to the window to gaze out at the night sky. Guilt racked his soul. "You damned us that night."

"I damned me," Nathan clarified as he reached for a full bottle of whiskey. "Your decision to cling to me is on you alone. I never asked for your presence nor do I welcome it." He glanced at the bed once more and then back at the mourning apparition. "Do you intend to stay and snivel or may I finally reflect in peace?"

"I am destined to stay," he answered softly. "You revel in

your kills, I mourn. For those you murder and for us."

"Suit yourself," Nathan chuckled. He opened the bottle and eased into the chair in front the fireplace. "Don't pray for them too hard, friend. Good girls don't end up in a predator's bed."

"Why I had to follow you on this hellish journey is beyond me," the ghost snapped. "The soul should have left the body when the last breath was taken."

"Heaven forbid I should be left to enjoy eternity in peace." Nathan's head fell back against the cushion. His eyes fell into a kind of trance as they watched the flames of the fire dance. "Why must I be the sole person to see you? Could you not attach yourself to someone who desires salvation?"

"It is not salvation I seek for us. It is an end."

Nathan drank deeply from the bottle and clutched it close to his chest. He closed his eyes, trying to escape the judgmental being who now shared every moment with him. Alcohol wouldn't drown it out completely but if he managed to swallow enough it would dull it for a time.

It had taken him quite a while to figure out that little trick. The woman who had turned him had been firm when she taught him how to survive as a vampire. Wine was necessary to lure prey sometimes, but it wouldn't serve much purpose past that. It just wasn't strong enough to provide the nourishment he needed to survive. Blood, she'd said, was the only thing that could. It alone would satisfy any craving he may have.

After years of listening to the ghost nag and whine, he'd drowned himself in a bottle of scotch and three bottles of the finest wine he could dig out of his cellar. The voice had mercilessly disappeared. He'd finally found peace. Better yet, when he woke the next night he didn't have a hangover.

Since then he'd kept his bar fully stocked. Only the finest. Only for him. Only for an escape. He had to be careful though. As with humans, alcohol thinned the blood. Not a good thing when your survival depends on that very substance. Tomorrow night he'd have to take two victims, perhaps three but he didn't care. Being alone in his own mind for a time was worth it.

As he looked out the window the ghost thought back to the night Nathan had accepted the vampire's "gift". Then he was only a small part of Nathan's subconscious mind, a part he would at times listen to. But that night he'd done his best to be heard. He told Nathan it was wrong. They'd be damned. They'd be no better than a parasite leeching off the living for survival. Nathan didn't care. The vampire's promise of immortality had been too good to resist.

Since then he'd been forced to witness horrible things. Why he didn't vanish when Nathan's heart stopped he didn't know, but he'd come to believe it was his punishment for failing to put him on the right track long before. A higher power telling him he now had to correct the wrong.

But how? How could he make a man who no longer cares regret anything he's done? Nathan simply dismissed him, mocked him. He didn't even see the ghost, the one piece of his soul, as a part of himself anymore. In Nathan's mind he was alone. His actions impacted him and him alone.

How wrong he was. Visions of Nathan's victims paraded through the ghost's mind. He was haunted by the faces, the fear, the pleas of mercy, the screams that reverberated through his mind. The memories of every life Nathan had touched were forever seared in the ghost's thoughts. In his mind there was no peace.

His gaze shifted to the chair in front of the fireplace. Nathan had already finished off one bottle of whiskey and had started on another. His eyes moved from the chair to the bed. The body of a once vibrant young woman still lay there. Never again would she see the light of day. Never again would she know how refreshing a cool breeze on a warm summer's day feels. Never would she be able to look at her children and reflect on memories of her own childhood.

His eyes closed as he tried to hold back the tears. So much sadness. So much pain. Not just for Nathan's victims, for him as well. Every time Nathan killed, the ghost could feel a piece of his soul die. He couldn't escape it like Nathan could escape him. Or could he?

He glided across the room toward the fireplace and stopped beside the chair to look down on Nathan. Still staring at the fire, Nathan didn't seem to notice his ghostly companion was there. The ghost put his transparent hand on Nathan's shoulder and waited for a reaction. When none came he settled in for a very long night.

"Must we do this again?" Nathan asked. His speech was slurred but he was far from drunk.

"You take pride in your work, do you not?"

"It doesn't bother me if that's what you mean. I do what I have to do to survive."

"What you have to do?" the ghost asked. He knelt down in front of the chair and stared straight into Nathan's pale blue eyes. He let himself weave into Nathan's mind while tricking him into thinking he was still kneeling before him. "Or what you want to do?"

"Does it really matter?" Nathan drained the bottle and got up to get a bottle of scotch from the mantle.

"It matters a great deal." The projected image of the ghost drifted to face him. "The blood you need. The lives you take are unnecessary."

Nathan glared up at him, fury burning in his eyes. "Where would they be if I let them live? Still on the streets. Still living in squalor. Still starving. You may not agree, but I have done those people a favor."

"Could you not invite them to stay on here? We have more than enough work. The few men you have murdered could be maintaining our property. Doing the things we no longer can. The women could be taking care of the household duties. Some I'm sure were good cooks. They could have been used in the kitchen to feed the help."

"Or they simply could have robbed me blind while I slept," Nathan retorted. "Never hire help you don't know. That's the first thing my father taught me."

"You have an advantage he did not." Nathan looked confused. "The power to get into their heads. Everything you need to know is there."

Nathan took another drink and collapsed back into his chair. He looked up at the ghost and shook his head.

"No, I'm better alone. If I let them live they'd know what I am."

"Do we not also possess the power of persuasion?" the ghost asked.

"I suppose," Nathan said thoughtfully. "Though it might

not work. Some minds are stronger than others."

"Could you not use those minds to your advantage also?"

"How?"

"The money our family left us will not last forever. Not many people do business at night. Gambling has proved lucrative so far, but there will come a day when the mind tricks won't work. Find a good mind, one good with figures and our wealth could last." Nathan stroked the dark stubble on his chin. "As I mentioned before, there is the matter of the grounds. They need tending. The house itself needs painting. If we had enough help we could plant crops. A good foreman could oversee all that."

"All good points," Nathan said. "But there is still that little matter of me being what I am. How do you propose I get them to look past that? I obviously can't alter their memories every night."

"Pay them well. Treat them well and it will not matter."

"And when I do kill. What then?"

"Don't kill. Take only what you need. It's that simple."

Nathan laughed and took another drink. He tossed the empty bottle on the floor where it shattered. "What good is being a predator when you can't kill prey? You fill my head with these ideas. Good ideas, I'll give you that. And then tell me I can't be what I was made to be? Have you lost your mind?"

"Simply thinking logically," the ghost answered. "If you have any hope of keeping everything we have now you must be willing to place your trust in others as well as make certain sacrifices of your own."

"You mean live my life the way you want me to."

"Just because you have the ability to be cruel and heartless doesn't mean we should," the ghost told him.

"Damn you!" Nathan yelled. He picked up the end table

beside his chair and threw it at the ghost. It crashed into the fireplace. "Ahh!!! I can't even- Damn you to hell!"

"You've already done that."

"I obviously haven't buried you far enough."

Nathan stomped out of the room, slamming the heavy door behind him unaware the ghost was still with him. Halfway down the hallway he looked over his shoulder expecting to be dogged further. To his surprise his depressing shadow was nowhere in sight. Relieved, he tromped down the stairs in need of something much stronger than what he usually kept in his room.

As soon as the bottle of Absinthe was in his hands he felt a sense of calm come over him. He hadn't had any in years, but he had a feeling it was exactly what he needed to completely silence the holier-than-thou voice he was so tired of hearing.

"Just one night," he said to bottle. "One night of peace is all I ask."

With that he popped the top and let the liquid roll down his throat. It was stronger, more bitter than he remembered. Had it sat too long? Ah, he didn't care. Shutting out the ghost was more important. He grabbed another bottle for good measure and went outside.

Though there wasn't a star in sight, the crisp night air felt good. The clouds suited his mood, he thought. Maybe they were just as tired of the bright, cheery stars as he was of that damn thing he'd left back in his room.

Nathan lifted his glass to the sky and tilted his head. "To silence," he whispered into the night. "May we all be granted a measure of peace."

"May we indeed," a woman's voice whispered.

Surprised, Nathan turned around to see who had joined him in the courtyard, but there was no one there. He squinted his eyes to look further out onto the property. Still nothing. Sure his mind was playing tricks on him, he settled into one of the chairs and drank a little more.

"You've forgotten me," the female voice whispered. Nathan whipped his head around. Nothing. Chills ran down his spine. "I was your first." He felt her cold breath on his neck. Frozen, he closed his eyes and willed the voice away. "No, I will not leave. I've been silent too long."

"Leave me!" he yelled.

"You will hear me," she whispered calmly. "You saved me. You tricked me. You seduced me. You forgot me. Now I'll make you remember me."

She made herself visible to him, a vision of beauty and grace. Long, curly blond hair. Her eyes were as bright as sapphires. Her lips as red as rubies. Skin like porcelain. She was young, maybe sixteen. Her body was perfect. Curvy; luscious. Exactly what a man desires. How could he have forgotten such a beauty?

"It's simple. You only saw me as you wanted to see me," she said. "Dirty, homeless, helpless, alone. I was a tool. I was there to satisfy you and nothing else. You used me. You ruined me and then you murdered me."

"Even under a mountain of filth I would have seen your beauty," he told her. "I'm afraid you have me mistaken with another."

She put her hand on his. His eyes rolled into the back of his head. Everything went black then there was a fuzzy image. He thought it was his mentor, but he couldn't be sure. Muffled voices echoed in his ears. As the image came into focus he realized she was showing him the night his mentor had left him.

He'd been furious when she left. She had promised to stay with him long enough to teach him everything he needed to know, but was gone within a month leaving him with only the basics to survive. Not to mention a few thousand dollars poorer. Payment for her trouble.

In an effort to quench his thirst for revenge he'd decided to seek out the most helpless soul he could find. He wanted to give her hope. Make her feel special. Make her think she could be part of his world and then squash her the way his mentor had done him.

Luckily for him, he didn't have to look far. He'd only been on his horse a short time when he came across the very thing he'd set out to find; huddled under a tree, downtrodden and filthy. Even when he jumped from his horse and knelt down beside her she refused to look up. She simply kept her eyes to the ground. Unfortunately her timid manner made her the perfect victim.

She removed her hand from his head. "Now that you know who I am, tell me why?"

He opened his eyes and turned his head to look at her. "What future did you have? I found you in the mud."

"You could have changed that," she said coolly.

"Why would I do that?" he snorted. "You chose your path. It was your foolish decision to leave your home. It was your decision to roam the countryside alone. Again, foolish. You yourself invited danger in."

"And you eagerly accepted."

The woman vanished leaving him alone with his bottle and his thoughts. Not that he dwelled on them long. As far as he

was concerned he was right. She was naïve to think she could survive on her own for long. If he hadn't come along and taken her in
someone else would have. And he doubted they would have been
as kind as he had been.

Nathan drained the bottle, tossed it aside and opened up
the second one. As he lay back in his chair enjoying the fresh air,
his mind drifted back to the young lady. She'd been so young, so
scared. Getting her on his horse had been hard. That had been
nothing compared to gaining her trust. That had definitely been a
game worth playing.

He'd offered her food, a warm place to spend the night.
On the promise of clean clothes, he'd managed to get her out of
her rags and into a much-needed bath. Looking back on the vision
of her wrapped in a blanket, her bare shoulders tempting him,
even he had to admit he'd missed exactly how beautiful she was
that night.

He took another drink and sank further into his memories.
Everything had been fine until he'd stated his price for his kind-
ness. By then though there was no escape. Whether she wanted
him or not, he would have her. And have her he did. Her cries
meant nothing to him. Her whimpers only fed his desire to dom-
inate her more. The power he felt in that moment was greater than
anything he had ever experienced before. And he wanted more.

Dawn had set upon them before he had finally decided to
put an end her miserable life; a more than satisfying kill. With her
death he knew what he was destined to be. Twisted as it was, he
saw himself as an angel of mercy.

"They should thank me," he mumbled.

"For what?" a deep voice growled.

Startled, Nathan's eyes shot open. Standing over him was

an almost transparent figure of a man. He jumped out of his chair, trying to regain his bearings.

The man was tall. His build more to the lean side, but Nathan could see just by looking at him that he was stout. No doubt due to years of manual labor. His hair was short and scruffy. A thick layer of stubble outlined his pale face.

"You look like you need this," the man said handing Nathan his bottle of absinthe. No less than half the bottle disappeared as soon as he had back in his hands. "Be warned, you won't find peace that way."

"Who says I'm looking for peace?" Nathan snorted.

"Aren't you?" The man moved closer, stopping mere inches from Nathan's face. Despite himself, Nathan flinched. "A man who kills as indiscriminately as you. I would think some kind of escape from the monster inside would be a blessing."

"Ha! The monster inside?" Nathan took another drink to steel his nerves and glanced back at the house. "That is the least of my worries." He looked over the man standing in front of him, finally recognizing him as a man he'd played cards with a year or so earlier. "If you are here to tell me how horrible your death was, save it. I know for a fact you went quickly."

"I did," he said. His deep voice cut through the still night like thunder. "My family did not."

"I fail to see how your family's suffering is my problem."

Before he knew what was happening Nathan found himself peering through a dark and dirty window. Snow covered the ground. Even he could feel the chill in the air. Inside the tiny house, the fire in the hearth wasn't much more than a smolder. He peered around the room. Huddled on a small bed in the corner was a young boy. His terrified eyes were fixed on a rocking chair sitting a few feet in front of him.

"My wife," the man beside him said. His voice was sad and hollow. "When I didn't come home she just wasted away." He touched the window, tears in his eyes. "My son was only five. For a week he sat in that same spot staring at his mother waiting for a miracle. Waiting for me to come and save them."

"And you blame me for that?" Nathan asked. He waved his hand as if to make the scene playing out before him disappear. "The weak woman was your choice, not mine."

"Weak?" the man roared. "Lily was far from weak."

"A woman who gives up her will to live simply because her husband vanishes is weak. She should have held her head high, thanked the powers that be that you died while she was still viable and looked for another to warm her bed."

"She had our son to think of."

"He would have adjusted. One man is as good as another." The man started to speak, but Nathan shook his head and continued. "Yes, yes...I know. You loved each other. A love so deep neither could possibly love another. Spare me. Love like that doesn't exist. It never has. Only fools believe it does. You should be thanking me for putting you all out of your misery."

Suddenly they were inside Nathan's living room, holding an empty bottle. The man pointed at a painting hanging over the mantle. The beautiful woman smiling down at them was Nathan's wife. She had died several years before, having succumbed to an illness the doctors couldn't diagnose.

"And her?" the man asked angrily. "You loved her dearly yet you tell me it doesn't exist?"

"Had she loved me at all she would still be here. When she gave up on life, she gave up on me."

The man stepped back. Pity replaced anger. He shook his head and began to fade away. "You are a selfish man."

"You think I care?"

"You should," he said softly. "You really should."

~*~

The ghost sighed. The two victims he'd thought he could use to reach Nathan had failed. The man no longer cared. His human side was truly dead. Tired and defeated, he allowed himself to drift out of Nathan's mind. Though the fight was far from over, he knew he'd need a new course of action.

The sound of fists pounding on wood and glass shattering jolted him out of his thoughts. Nathan had hit the mantle so hard his hands were bleeding. For the first time in ages he had tears in his eyes. He reached up to touch the portrait above him and sank to the cold floor, trembling.

Nathan sat on the floor; his shoulders slumped, staring up at the portrait of his wife. Tears were rolling down his cheeks. He looked more human to the ghost now than he had in the months before he had been turned. He looked sick as well. The robust tone of his skin had faded to a cool gray. His pale blue eyes now even paler. Something had broken inside him. Something the ghost had completely missed.

Perplexed, the ghost fought the urge to strike, to use Nathan's sudden onset of emotion against him. Better to let this play out without his interference. Especially if there was a higher power at play.

"You left me!" Nathan screamed at the portrait. "I begged you to stay with me yet you left. You knew how much I loved you. You knew how much I needed you."

The room fell silent. The ghost watched wide-eyed as Nathan wailed on the ground like a spoiled toddler. He'd never seen a break like this before. Not even when he'd held her hand as she died. He couldn't be bothered with words of love and grief before and during her funeral. He'd been unable to shed a tear when they put her in the ground. While friends and family wept, he had held his head low, devoid of all emotion.

Or so they'd thought. Only he and the ghost, then a small part of Nathan's soul, knew his true feelings then. The feelings only displayed in quiet thoughts or angry moments spent alone. He'd lost count of the number of glasses, furniture, and clothes that had to be replaced after having one of his fits. That said, fits of that magnitude had become rare since the night he'd been turned.

Nathan wiped his nose on his sleeve and crawled over to the cabinet on the far side of the room. He swung open the door and got out a bottle of bourbon. He scooted back against the wall, held the bottle up to the portrait and bowed his head.

"Cheers," he mumbled.

Time ticked by as the ghost watched Nathan crumble even more. Though words stopped, the tears continued to flow. More than once he had felt an odd tingle in his head. Probably the ghost trying to get in, but he was so overcome by emotion he no longer cared.

"Get up, boy," a rough, husky voice growled. In an instant he was by Nathan's side. Solidarity, no matter how strained their relationship had become, was understood when dealing with Nathan's father. Alive or dead, Henry was a force to be reckoned with. "You heard me, boy. Get off the floor and act like the man I raised you to be."

Nathan looked around the room, searching for the source of the voice. The ghost did too.

"On your feet, son!" the voice boomed.

Nathan sat up, but couldn't get to his feet. He shook his head as if to shake the voice away. Without warning he found himself up against the wall, his feet dangling two feet above the ground. The collar of his shirt was pulled tight around his neck as if a hand had grabbed and twisted it. His eyes shifted toward the ghost who could only shrug in answer to his unspoken question.

Nathan's eyes widened, yet there was still no visible trace of the man behind the cool voice.

"My legacy," Henry said coolly. Nathan fell back to the floor. "My son. A pitiful excuse for a man. Never in my life have I seen a man as cowardly as you." Nathan slowly dropped his head following the sound of the disembodied voice. "You had a fine wife. A beautiful house any man would be proud to call home. Fortune enough to live the rest of your life in comfort. All you needed to do was hire the right men. Yet you let it all go to waste."

"I did no-" he protested.

"Silence!" Henry yelled. "You've destroyed my name. You've destroyed my home. You've destroyed my business. All that I worked for GONE. How long do you think the money you inherited will last?" Nathan tried to answer, but was cut off before he could. "It won't. It won't because you haven't maintained the fields. How long has it been since they last produced a crop? I thought after the death of your wife you would have at least tried to fill your time with work. It would have been a welcome distraction from the guilt you most surely felt."

"Guilt?" Nathan asked. The drunken fog he'd been in

seemed to disappear. "What in the hell would I have to feel guilty for?"

"You killed her. We all know it."

"Me?!" Nathan yelled. "She's the one who got sick, not me. She's the one who wouldn't get well, not me."

"You neglected her early on. She had been sick for months. We all saw it, but she was your wife, your responsibility. Had you opened your eyes and seen someone besides yourself maybe you would still have a life."

Disbelief then anger flashed through Nathan's eyes. He scrambled to his feet. Apparently prepared for a face off. "A life, Father? I do have a life. A very good life in case you haven't noticed. I have everything I need. Money, a home, and time."

"A lonely life, limited money, and too much time," his father's voice said. "You're a disappointment. You always have been. I should have drowned you like a rat when you were born. I knew even then you'd be worthless. If your mother hadn't already lost two children before you I would have."

Tears stung Nathan's eyes. Silence took the place of words. The ghost stayed still, waiting for one or the other to hurl an insult. None came. Nathan dropped back to the floor, his hands pulling hard at his hair. His body shook. He let out a frustrated scream and looked at the cabinet.

"To hell with you!" he screamed, reaching for another bottle. "Do you hear me? TO HELL WITH YOU!"

He froze. A cold breeze hit them full on. Lavender perfume wafted through the air around them. Tears rolled down Nathan's cheeks. His head tilted to the side, eyes closed as if a hand was cradling it.

"Did he send you?" Nathan asked.

"No, I came on my own," a woman's voice answered. Like Henry, she was invisible. "You need not listen to him, Nate. He expects too much of you. He always has."

"He said I killed her." His voice cracked. "Did I? Did I miss something? Did I not see what everyone else did?"

"You saw only what you wanted to see, Nate," she answered, her voice barely a whisper. "That's all you've ever seen."

His body tensed. "So you agree?"

"Not entirely, but yes."

He grabbed another bottle and stomped across the room. The ghost felt her move with him, but still couldn't see her. He didn't know her voice, but whoever she was had a power over Nathan no one else ever could. He could feel Nathan's anger bubbling under the surface, but something about this woman kept that anger at bay.

"If I am nothing more than a murderer, why are you here?"

"I never said you murdered her," she said gently. "We both know you're a selfish man. We both know you weren't as attentive as you could have been. That's not the same thing as killing her. Besides, you know how I feel about her. She was too fragile for you."

"Be careful," he warned.

"I know you loved Sarah, but you loved yourself more. You've always loved yourself more."

The ghost felt the air in the room shift. He looked to Nathan. "Is she gone?"

"You tell me," Nathan mumbled. He turned on his heel and left the room already working on emptying the bottle in his hand.

The ghost followed him up the stairs and into his room. Nathan was leaning against the doorway, staring at the bed. "Why Karen?" he asked. "Of all the people you could have dug up, why did you have to bring her?"

"Pardon me?" the ghost asked.

"Don't play dumb. I know that was you."

"The woman downstairs?" Nathan nodded. "That wasn't me."

"No? Then who? I sure as hell didn't do it."

"You must have, because I didn't. I don't even know who she is."

"How could you not? Karen was Sarah's younger sister. Don't you remember? She used to pursue me like a bitch in heat."

The ghost searched his memory, but still came up empty. "I'm sorry, but I don't know who she is."

Nathan started laughing. The ghost could only stare. "I'll be damned. She said once she could make me forget everything. I guess she was right."

"You were lovers?" No matter how hard he tried he couldn't remember her.

"You could say that, but love never had a place in our relationship," he chuckled. "It's a shame you don't remember." He took another drink, put the bottle down on the mantle and walked over to the bed. A mischievous smile spread across his lips. "There were many nights she kept me satisfied when Sarah couldn't." He frowned and glanced back at the ghost. "Maybe that's why you don't remember her. There was always a piece of myself I never could let Karen touch. Maybe that piece was you."

"How could you?" the ghost asked. Disgust rang in his

voice.

"How could I?" Nathan chuckled. "It was simple. She wanted me. Who was I to say no?"

"You were married."

"Not at first," he confessed. "Karen came to me a year before Sarah and I wed."

"Yet you married her?"

"The best of both worlds my friend." Nathan pushed the curtain above the bed aside. The night sky was beginning to fade. He turned to face the ghost and continued, "On one hand, I had an angel I loved with all my heart. On the other, I had a devil I could use at my disposal."

The ghost could take no more. Nathan had betrayed his wife in the worst possible way. Both before and after they were married. He'd shamed two families as well. Whether either family knew it or not, he was sure others did. Back then there were eyes all over the farm. For all he knew, Sarah had found out about Nathan's affair and died of a broken heart.

That thought elevated Nathan's betrayal to a whole new level. He gathered his energy and grabbed the bottle from the mantle. The glass shattered over Nathan's head. Bits of glass cut into his skull. Blood poured from the cuts and gashes. Thanks to all the alcohol he'd consumed his blood was thin and he passed out.

While he had the energy and opportunity, the ghost went out in search of rope. He was going to end this tonight. He may not have been able to appeal to Nathan's human side, but that didn't matter anymore. He'd hurt too many people. Letting him live was no longer an option.

He hurried out to the barn to find the strongest rope he

could find. It didn't take long to decide to use leather instead. It was stronger and it was right there. Before he left the barn he opened the stalls to let the horses out. After tonight there would be no one left to feed them. At least this way they wouldn't starve.

He drifted back up the stairs relieved to find Nathan still passed out on the floor. The ghost brought in a wooden chair from the room next door and deposited Nathan's limp body into it. Once there he secured his limbs. Both hands were tied to the arms of the chair at his wrists while his ankles were strapped to the legs.

While he waited for Nathan to come to he went downstairs to get the portrait of Sarah. It was high time Nathan faced her.

He placed the frame at the foot of the bed. The chair he'd put in the center of the room. The sun would rise soon and for the first time in years the curtains would be drawn.

The ghost looked to the dead woman on the bed and said a quick prayer. He placed a hand on her head and said, "Please forgive me for leaving you here like this."

"She's dead, you idiot," Nathan mumbled. His head rolled from one side to the other. "I doubt she cares."

"Her soul may," the ghost said solemnly.

Nathan tried to move his arm. He couldn't. He shook his head as if trying to clear his head. The ghost knelt down beside him, pointing out the leather bindings.

"You've taken your last life," the ghost told him.

"I haven't even begun," Nathan said defiantly. He wiggled his arms trying to loosen the bindings. "I'm a vampire. These won't hold me for long."

"That might be true—normally. But tonight you've had quite a bit to drink. Your blood is thin. The cuts on your head have yet to heal. In fact they are still bleeding. I doubt you'll get loose in time."

"In time for what?" Nathan noticed the portrait of Sarah at the foot of the bed. Again tears stung his eyes. This time though he fought to keep them back. Survival was more important. "Answer me!"

The ghost drew the curtains. Nathan sat unblinking at the pink tinged sky. A sight he hadn't seen in years. Then it hit him. The sun.

"Untie me! Untie me now!"

"No," the ghost said. "Your reign of terror is over."

"I die, you die." He pulled at the bindings even harder. Panic gripped him. He tried kicking his feet loose, but his head was too fuzzy and the room started to spin.

"I welcome it," the ghost whispered. His energy finally spent, he faded back into the shadows of the room. The sun was rising fast now. Peace was within reach.

Nathan's eyes darted from the portrait of his wife to the rising sun. It wasn't yet high enough to light the room. Maybe just maybe the window would offer a layer of protection.

"Your time has come, my love," a soft voice whispered. Nathan felt Sarah's lips brush against his ear, but she remained invisible to him. He closed his eyes, hoping this was all a dream. "You've hurt so many people, Nathan."

"Show yourself." He opened his eyes. She wasn't there. The sky was brighter now. He could feel the sun's heat as it began to warm up the room. Desperation took hold. "Sarah, please! Help me. Don't let me die this way."

"There is nothing I can do," she whispered. "This was your doing, not mine."

"If you ever loved me, you'd help me." He fought against the bindings but they refused to give. The light was moving closer. "Sarah! I'm your husband! Get me loose!"

"You were never mine."

The window blew open. A rush of sunlight poured in. Something pushed his chair closer. Scared, he searched the room for anything, anyone that could help. There was nothing. He tried to clear his head, but he couldn't. Too much alcohol. Too much fear and too many thoughts.

The smell of burning flesh started to fill his nostrils. He looked down to see his hands, feet and legs smoking. Pain like he'd never felt before racked his body. He opened his mouth to scream, but no sound came out. The pain moved throughout his body. It sat there, burning, tearing through his organs until he felt like his body would split in half. After what felt like hours his skin began to flake away. His life was finally over.

IN THE RED

Quincy J. Allen

4:47pm - December 5th, 1897

Wind clawed at my face and chewed into my fingers like a rabid dog.

God damn Chicago winters, I thought as I shrugged deeper into my coat. I pulled the collar up around my ears in a vain attempt to keep out the biting cold. I could almost hear the wind laughing at me.

They tell rookies to jam their hands under their armpits and stamp their feet when it's cold.

Bullshit.

I'm no rookie, and nothing keeps out Chicago wind except brick walls and steam heating, and then... *maybe.* I've hated Windy City winters since I was a kid, but it's the best place in the world to be a cop. There's just no end of gangsters and corrupt politicians. And damn near every cop in Chicago is either taking money to look the other way or flat-out working for those very same gangsters and corrupt politicians.

It makes a guy like me feel like I'm worth something...

even when everybody else—including my captain—thinks I should have been a priest.

I turned back towards the precinct and grumbled. What the hell else could I do? A safe house and two ill-tempered cops waited to be relieved, but Seamus had cornered yet another victim. This time it was Mrs. O'Toole with a rump roast and a sack of potatoes slung over her shoulder. Although she ran the local numbers and off-track betting racket, she still did her own grocery shopping and cooking. Tough as nails and frequently as means as a snake, that one.

Her back was to me, but there was no mistaking the gray coif piled on top of her head. She was also the only Irishwoman in the ward who strolled about in a red plaid long coat with bandy, seemingly cold-impervious legs sticking out the bottom. She probably had a billy-club hidden in her jacket somewhere.

I glanced at my pocket watch and realized we were going to be late. O'Connell and Reardon, the waiting cops, were going to bitch like Temperance League spinsters when we walked through the door.

Every cop in the precinct hated safe house duty. We never knew who we were protecting, or why. And safe houses usually had paper-thin walls and undersized wood-burners. It meant hours spent in cold apartments with nothing to do but watch paint peel and listen to people bitch about how cold it was.

Another gust from the north raced down the street between two-story row houses, kicking up ice that raked across my exposed skin like sandpaper. Swirls of white faded into alleys deep with drifts. I turned my back into the wind and blew into cupped palms.

"Seamus!" I shouted.

He glanced at me over Mrs. O'Toole's potato sack and nodded. "Yeah! I'm coming!"

Seamus O'Malley—we'd been best friends since before we could walk. We'd saved each other's necks more times than I could count, and he was the only man in Chicago I trusted with my life.

There were only two cops in the precinct who didn't think Seamus O'Malley was dirty. The first, of course, was Seamus himself. To hear him tell the tale, he was as pure as the driven snow that covered Chicago. He told that story to anyone he could corner, and I must admit, he was right, but you have to understand Chicago snow.

Coal plants had turned the buildings, the trees, the sky… even the *people* gray. Hell, snow hadn't been white in Chicago since Seamus and I were kids picking our noses on the south side.

The other cop who didn't consider Seamus dirty was me.

Chicago cops are a lot like a pile of dirty laundry. Most are dirty, as in covered in shit one way or another, but Seamus is like one of those shirts on top. Sure, it doesn't smell like spring, but you could wear it again if you had to. Not dirty, just not clean either.

As for me, I actually am the only cop in our precinct who isn't on the take. Hell, I might be the only cop in Chicago who doesn't earn a little extra on the side by looking the other way.

Seamus nodded again to Mrs. O'Toole, handed her something—*Probably a bet,* I thought— and then moved around her, quick-stepping towards me. His thin frame looked bulky inside a gray Norfolk coat, presumably layered underneath with any wool he could get his hands on. His red hunter's cap, flaps down over his ears, covered a thick crown of wiry, red hair. He was taller than me, but I weighed more on account of my thicker frame. He'd resented that since our school days, especially when I gave him grief about blowing away in the next strong breeze.

"You tell her how good a cop you are?" I asked, chuckling as he got within earshot.

"What?" He looked confused for a second. "Oh, yeah, yeah. That. I gave her the same old story." He pulled on my arm and turned me down the street. "It's cold, Billy-boy. Lemme buy you a cup of coffee."

"What?" I looked at him like he was crazy. "We're gonna be late."

"Them boys will wait for us." He tugged on my arm again. "Besides, you look chilled to the bone."

"I am, but—"

"Trust me, Billy-boy." He patted his chest where he always kept a flask. "Maybe we'll add a little Irish whiskey to the coffee to keep us from freezing to death." He stepped behind me, gently guiding me over a snow berm and onto the street. The steamplows, new to Chicago, had done a great job keeping the main thoroughfares clear, but high ridges of packed snow flowed over onto the sidewalks throughout most of the city.

I could tell Seamus was aiming me at a diner on the corner. "Besides, it's not like Reardon and O'Malley are going to bitch any less if we're twenty-five minutes late instead of only five." He stopped short in the middle of the street and turned me to face him, looking serious. "I'll make you a deal. Let me buy you a cup of Joe with a wee dram of Irish whiskey, and I'll give up telling people how good a cop I am for a whole week." He smiled, a mischievous glint in his eye. Then he winked once. He'd been doing that to me my whole life… a deal and a wink… over and over again. Most of the time he came up short on his deals, and he generally reneged. But what are friends for?

"You drive a hard bargain," I replied, smiling. "I'm gonna hold you to this one, you know." I always said that, but I never really did.

"So, we have a deal?"

"Deal," I said, shaking my head.

He almost looked relieved.

We made it into the diner without freezing to death, and I made good on my half of the bargain. But I didn't stop looking at my pocket watch, and I got us moving as quickly as possible.

~*~

The apartment building was only ten years old, but everything in that part of town looked weathered and beat to hell. The boards creaked as we made our way up three flights of dingy stairwell. Old sweat and older vegetables tainted air cold enough to show our breath.

The precinct sure does know how to take care of witnesses in style, I thought.

Seamus topped the landing and stepped up to the door with a faded 301 painted on it. He knocked three times, then once, then twice.

"Hey, boyos!" he called out. "The A-team is here!" Seamus turned to me and winked, smiling at his jab.

The door opened quickly, but I couldn't see who stood in the doorway. As Seamus turned his head, I heard a sharp *POP!*

The back of Seamus' head came apart before my eyes.

Blinded by a spray of blood, I was too shocked to move. Burning pain streaked across my cheek as the bullet that killed Seamus grazed me. I staggered back.

Oh God! was all I had time to think as another dull *POP!* filled the stairwell.

The bullet slammed into my shoulder like a sledgehammer, spinning me around, pushing me over the top step. Pain blossomed like fireworks as I tumbled down the stairs. I hit the lower landing face first with a shuddering *SMACK!* My head swam. The cold boards felt like ice beneath my cheek, and my legs stretched out partway up the stairs. For a few seconds the whole of my world was cold floor, blood, and pain. I heard heavy footsteps thump down the stairs and pause.

POP! POP!

I shuddered with the impact of two more slugs. Agony coursed through my lower back.

Paralyzed by fear and pain, I saw the blurry shape of my killer step past me and run down the stairs. Through a haze of crimson, all I could make out was a black and gray wash of clothing topped by a derby. And then he was gone.

I felt blood seeping from my face and shoulder, pooling on the floor around my cheek and already growing cold.

I closed my eyes and waited to die.

~*~

I'm lying face up in a snow bank. I'm naked. The sky is a featureless gray, and wind-swirls full of white flakes dance above me. I try to rise out of the snow, but I can't.

Fear.

Looking down, I see that my legs are mostly covered. My feet mostly poke out through the white. My arms are nearly covered, and there's a thin layer of snow across my chest. I'm not cold though, which seems very strange.

I hate the cold.

I realize the wind isn't making any sound. In fact, nothing is except my own, slow breathing. The silence presses in on me, but it seems perfectly natural somehow.

Time passes, although I can't say how much. My arms are now covered, and only my toes poke through a swell of snow. My chest is nearly covered. I know time is running out, but for what I don't know.

And I don't care.

There just doesn't seem to be a point.

The silence is broken by the crunch of footsteps in snow... coming from my right.

Seamus slowly comes into view, looking down at me. He's naked too, and there's a bullet-hole over his right eye.

He looks worried.

He says something, but I can't hear him. His worry turns to anger. He shouts at me, again and again, but it only comes through as a dull muffle, like wind brushing against a thick windowpane. All I can do is stare at him, and for some reason I wish he would go away.

He stops shouting, and I notice tears running down his cheeks.

He turns his gaze up to the gray sky. I see him shouting again and can hear more dull muffles, but I can't tell what he's saying. He raises his fist, shaking it in fury.

Then I see it.

Above us, dancing and flittering around amidst the swirls of wind and snow, is a small piece of paper half the size of a dollar bill. When it comes within reach, Seamus plucks it from the air. He looks down at it briefly, nods once, and then folds it up.

He kneels down next to me. I hear his knee settle near my head. He brushes the snow off my chest and gives me a reassuring smile. He lifts my arm, brushing away the snowflakes, and holds my hand in front of my face. He gently places the paper into my palm and closes my fin-

gers around it, looking intently into my eyes. He nods once, squeezes my fist, and lays my hand back down gently.

Then he closes his eyes, and I can see him breathing deeply, as if he's concentrating, summoning his strength for something.

His eyes shoot open. He raises his hand high. It comes down hard and fast in a sweeping arc, slapping me across the face. I feel the pain, and it courses through my entire body like a lightning bolt.

"WAKE UP!" he shouts.

The gray sky, the white snow, and Seamus… they all turn to black.

~*~

I woke with a start and opened my eyes to a high ceiling of rough planks and cobweb-dusted crossbeams. The room was warm, and the green blanket covering me had raised beads of perspiration on my forehead. A generator hummed quietly somewhere above me, and the faint hiss of electricity sparked and crackled in an unsteady rhythm. Although I couldn't be certain, I had the sense that I was underground. Machine oil and the acrid taint of welded metal filled the air.

I lay upon a narrow bed set against a yellowed pattern of fleur-de-lis wallpaper mottled brown by water stains. A strange machine with two copper cylinders atop a wide framework squatted at the foot of the bed, gurgling and humming in a pulsing. The machine had several flexible tubes running from the cylinders to disappear under the blanket between my feet.

I felt something in my hand and raised it up from under the blanket. It looked like the piece of paper from my dream. I unfolded it and recognized it instantly. But it didn't make any sense, so I folded it again and tried to figure out what the hell had happened to me.

My memories were a jumble of images that took seconds to congeal into anything meaningful. And then it hit me: the stairwell... the door... the *gunshots*.

"Oh, Seamus," I said quietly.

The sound of a tool being placed gently upon a workbench caught my ear. I turned my head sideways.

He was a small man with a wild ring of salt-and-pepper hair around a barren crown, and the linen shirt and tweed trousers seemed to cover an almost skeletal frame. He had an oil-stained smock over his clothing, and it seemed a size or two too large for him. I would guess he was in his fifties, but he had the wrinkles of someone much older with the eyes of a child. A set of dark goggles lay draped around his bird-like neck.

"Good, you're awake," he said in a pinched, Welsh accent. "You've been asleep for quite a while."

He leaned against a workbench covered with tools, brass housings, and machine parts. Their surfaces gleamed in the lamplight. Beside the bench stood a seven-foot mannequin of bronze, with dim yellowish eyes. The mannequin had a large, plate housing for its torso, with thick housing for shoulders and thighs. It had heavy, wrist-thick struts for its forearms and shins, and its joints appeared to rotate around polished gears driven by gleaming pistons. Its arms terminated in four-digit hands with opposable thumbs.

Beside the mannequin sat a narrow wheelchair that seemed to have been homemade but clearly crafted by the same hand as the mannequin.

"How long?" I asked.

"It's March seventeenth... Saint Patrick's Day... which I find rather interesting considering your name... Mr. Patrick."

Lifting my head off the pillow, I said tersely, "Who are y —?"

But he cut me off with a raised hand. "You can't get up, so don't try." His tone was soft, almost apologetic.

"Am I a prisoner?" I asked, fearful and angry. I had no idea what sort of trouble I might be in.

Again, he had an apologetic tone. "Quite the opposite, Mr. Patrick. When I say you can't get up, it's because I mean you are not capable of the feat."

"What do you mean?" I asked angrily.

He sighed and stole his eyes away from mine. He looked around the room, as if he were looking for the answer to my question. Finally, he locked eyes with me and said, "Wiggle your feet."

I looked at the bumps of my toes beneath the blanket, trying to do as he asked.

Nothing happened.

It was then that I realized I'd only felt the bed beneath me from my buttocks up. There was no sensation below that. Anguish filled me… threatened to tear me apart.

"Oh, God," I whispered. I squeezed my eyes shut and felt tears streaming down my temples into the pillow.

"You're lucky to be alive," he soothed. "If it weren't for the cold in that stairwell slowing everything down, you'd have bled to death."

"So the cold kept me alive, did it?" I said quietly. Whatever dislike I'd had for winter blossomed into seething hatred. I turned to the wall, holding back the sobs pulling at my insides. "You should have let me die."

He sighed again. "I had hoped, Mr. Patrick, that you would be the sort of man who would want to find your friend's killer. And in doing so, find the man who killed my brother."

Confusion broke through the waves of self-pity washing over me, and I turned to him. "Seamus was your brother?"

"No. My brother was the witness your precinct was tasked with protecting. A task which fell woefully short of the mark."

"I don't even know who it was."

"His name was Bowen Nash-Davies... my younger brother." The man's voice was full of sadness and regret. I could tell that something weighed heavily upon him. He smiled weakly. "My brother was an accountant by trade, and it seems he got involved with the wrong people... *yet again*." He shook his head, and a resigned sigh deflated the man's narrow frame. He stared at the floor for long moments.

"Sir?" I asked to break him of his reverie.

"Oh!" He squared his shoulders and looked at me. "Yes, of course. Where are my manners? You are not in my employ, so we'll have to do away with that 'Sir' nonsense. I know who *you* are, so permit me to introduce myself. I am I am Professor Gaius Nash-Davies, at your service. Now let's see what we can do about getting you out of that bed and moving."

"I thought you said I wasn't capable of the feat."

"Well," he gave me a thoughtful look, "I did say that, but I meant that you would not be able to do so on your own. I built this chair and my friend here," he bent his head towards the mannequin, "to give you a more reasonable sense of mobility." He smiled with a bit of pride. "Please remove that blanket and undo the strap across your hips." Without another word he turned to the mannequin and bent down behind its legs.

As I pulled the blanket back, I saw him pull a cable out of the mannequin's heel. He stepped behind the thing and opened a panel in its back.

Beneath the blanket I discovered I was wearing a long nightshirt that had been split up the back and tied behind my neck. The shirt covered down to my knees, and the tubes from the machine at the foot of the bed disappeared under it.

"What are these tubes for?" I asked a bit uncomfortably.

He peeked around the machine. "One has fed you during your sleep, and the other evacuated urine. A mechanism beneath the bed evacuated and disposed of more… err… substantial waste." Disappearing once again behind the mannequin, he said, "On the nightstand above your head you'll find a bit of cotton and a strip of gauze. Retrieve them, remove the needle connected to your inner-thigh, and apply the cotton and gauze to staunch any bleeding. Then remove the sheath from your… err… privates." He cleared his throat a bit uncomfortably.

With only a little bit of effort, I did as he instructed, tossing the tubing atop the machine at my feet.

"I'm done," I said.

"Good." He peeked from around the mannequin again, grinning. "Because so am I."

I heard the *CLICK* of a switch, and the mannequin's eyes lit up, glowing brightly. There was a whirring sound from within its torso, and it occurred to me that it might not just be something to hang clothes on.

"What is that thing?"

"Genius," he said gleefully, "in a brass casing." He closed the panel in its back and stepped around. "Jeeves, move wheel-chair to bed," the Professor said quietly.

"*Un—der—stood,*" it said in a buzzing, metallic voice. It slowly turned, placed its hands on the grips of the wheelchair, and started moving towards me with thumping steps, whining gears, and hissing pistons.

"Jesus!" I shouted. *The thing was alive!*

It stopped with the chair only inches from the edge of the bed.

"Jeeves, turn chair a quarter-turn right."

"*Un—der—stood.*" It moved the chair as directed.

"Jeeves," the Professor said, "move to bed and extend right arm."

"*Un—der—stood.*" And it did.

At first I thought the thing was going to fall on top of me, but it held steady.

"Unbelievable," I whispered.

The professor looked at me hopefully. "Mr. Patrick, do you think you could pull yourself up to a sitting position by grabbing onto its arm? Just dangle your legs over the bed.

I looked at him nervously. "I'm not sure I—"

"Just give it a try, Mr. Patrick. I'm sure it will take a little practice, but it's either this or you stay in a bed for the rest of your life." His face was resolute. "It's your choice."

I thought about it. There was a part of me that just wanted to lay there and die. Living life as a cripple terrified me, but something my grandfather told me took hold. When I was a lad he had spoken of William of Orange, a distant ancestor, whose motto had been, *While we breathe, we hope.*

Well, I was still breathing, so I reached up and grabbed hold of Jeeves' arm. Its limbs whined and hissed as I pulled, but the thing held steady. It took me a bit to shift my legs over the edge of the bed, but I eventually got into a sitting position. That's when I noticed the hole in the bed where my ass had been and a conveyor belt beneath.

"Well done," the Professor said. "Now raise your arms slightly."

I looked at him and cocked an eyebrow up. "What do you have in mind?"

"You'll see," he replied easily.

I raised my arms out a bit.

"Jeeves, place Mr. Patrick in wheelchair."

"Now wait a minute!" I shouted, but Jeeves ignored me.

With more piston-hissing and gear-whining, it moved its hands under my arms, squeezed gently, and lifted me up like I was a ragdoll. Before I knew it, I was sitting in the wheelchair, staring up at the machine. Its eyes still glowed a steady, bright yellow as it stared straight ahead.

"Where'd you get that?" he asked, staring at the floor in front of me.

"Get what?"

He pointed at the piece of paper I had dropped when I was picked up.

"Umm…. It was in my hand when I woke up. I was going to ask *you* where it came from."

"I don't know. It wasn't in your hand when I laid you out," he said, a bit perplexed.

"But—" I started. I remembered the dream… and Seamus. *It couldn't possibly be,* I thought. I looked at the Professor a bit nervously. "I had a dream…."

"A dream, eh?" Perplexed morphed on his face into intrigued. "Curious." His eyes narrowed and shifted left and right, and he seemed to be pondering possibilities. He appeared to finally settle something in his head and smiled at me.

"You don't believe me," I said.

"I neither believe nor disbelieve, Mr. Patrick. I'm an engineer and a scientist. That piece of paper was not in your hand when I had you brought here. I did not put it there. And you could not have gotten it on your own. Yet, it exists. Therefore, what either of us *believes* is irrelevant. Yes? In the absence of a reasonable explanation, we are left with the unreasonable. Would you like to tell me about your dream?"

I licked my lips, wondering if I did. Finally I said, "I don't think so." I was unnerved by the whole thing. The possibilities scared the hell out of me, and I didn't want to talk about it. Besides, he might think I was crazy.

He shrugged. "Suit yourself. Is anything written on the paper?"

I nodded. "It's half of a numbers ticket, with two of the three numbers, the date for the day before I was shot, and half of my partner's signature."

"Well, it seems you may have your first clue in solving the murders of Seamus and my brother. We may yet see some justice done."

~*~

I spent the next two days getting used to the wheelchair and ordering Jeeves around. The wheelchair was trickier than I would have thought, and it couldn't make it up the stairs that led out of the warehouse basement he lived in, but Jeeves solved that problem. It could lift the chair and collapse the frame inwards a few inches on each side, even with me in it. Then he would simply carry me up or down as needed. Despite my initial anxiety, I came to think of Jeeves as a complete marvel.

It could move about for hours at a time and recharge itself

by sticking its finger in just about any light-socket. Commanding Jeeves was quite simple. It understood a slew of nouns and verbs, and the Professor showed me how to teach it new ones.

The Professor—I came to call him Gaius—and I became fast friends, although he generally kept a wide physical space between us, which I thought was a bit peculiar. We ate our meals together at opposite ends of the table and talked about where we had come from. I spoke of Chicago, and he spoke of growing up in Britain.

His father had been an explorer of some renown and left them a healthy inheritance upon his passing. Shortly thereafter, he and his brother had come to America to ply their distinct trades. Gaius also implied more than once that his brother Bowen had a knack for getting in with the seedier aspects of society, performing *creative* accounting for them. It was a common enough practice in Britain, and Bowen had apparently found even more fertile soil in the Windy City.

On the third morning, as I was getting dressed, Gaius gently knocked on the door. I rolled over and opened it, rolling back quickly to respect the gap he preferred to keep between us. He stepped into the small bedroom he had provided me, looking both pensive and hopeful.

"I think it's time for you to set out, William," he said quietly.

"You're not coming with me?" I asked, somewhat surprised.

"I'm afraid I can't." He seemed embarrassed. "As you may have noticed, I have… specific… personal space issues." He wrung his hands together as he spoke. "You see, I have severe Anthropophobia."

"Anthro....po... what?" I'd never heard the term before.

"A severe fear of people." He smiled weakly. "I don't leave this place unless I absolutely have to, and then only within the confines of a sealed conveyance. It took a Herculean effort to bring you here, but I needed you. You're my only hope. You can go where I cannot. *Do* what I cannot."

It all fell into place. Why he lived in a basement. Why he had kept his distance during my time there. The Professor needed me to find his brother's killer. The precinct probably stopped looking before Seamus' body was cold, and Gaius suffered a self-imposed imprisonment. I nodded. "I understand."

"Do you know where you're going?" he asked.

I nodded again and pulled out the piece of paper I'd kept tucked away in my shirt pocket. "Mrs. Maggie O'Toole's home. I've been thinking about that dream. Seamus was in it. I think he wanted me to do something... and he gave me this to point me in the right direction."

Gaius nodded. "There is one last thing I want to show you."

I looked at him quizzically as he stepped up to Jeeves. He pressed twice on the outside of the machine's leg, and a panel swung open. He pulled out a rather strange looking, blocky device that reminded me of a pistol, but like no pistol I had ever seen.

"What the hell is that?" I asked.

"More genius," he said mischievously. "It's a magnetic pistol." He handed it to me.

"A what?" I gave it a close inspection. The thing was heavy. There was a grip and a trigger, but atop that was a wide block of metal about eight inches long, three inches wide, and an inch thick. It had a dime-sized hole in the end and two metal rods stuck out another two inches on either side of the hole. At the back of the thing was a copper cylinder with wires poking out that disappeared into small sockets along the main housing.

"Mag-pistol for short. It holds six copper slugs, and when you pull the trigger a strong electrical current travels along the barrel, accelerating a slug to a high velocity… much higher than the service revolver I presume you used to carry."

"I sure am glad you're on my side," I said, marveling at the weapon. I handed it back to him.

He chuckled and then returned it to Jeeves' thigh, closing the panel. "There's a pistol in each thigh, and they charge whenever Jeeves does. Hopefully you won't have to use one of those things, but it's nice to know they're nearby."

"Can't argue with that."

"Are you ready?"

"As I'm going to be," I replied a bit nervously. I was somewhat anxious about moving around Chicago in a wheelchair with Jeeves trailing behind me.

"I've arranged for a steam-truck to take you wherever you need to go. I would have called for a steam-carriage, but I believe your chair and Jeeves' weight would prove to be problematic."

"Thank you, Gaius…" I smiled humbly. "For *everything*." I owed my life to the man. "I don't know how I could ever repay you."

"If you solve my brother's murder, I'd consider us even, William."

I nodded.

"Jeeves," I said, looking up at the motionless machine by the door, "Take me upstairs."

With a whoosh of steam and a clatter of pistons, the truck came to an easy stop.

"Jeeves," I said, "open doors." The truck rocked as the machine stepped to the door with me close behind. It twisted a latch and pushed the doors open. I told it to get out and then grab the wheelchair as I rotated my back to him.

It swung me out, and Mrs. O'Toole's home came into view. It was a beautiful, two-story home set apart from the others on the block. The shrubs outside were manicured, and neatly swept steps led up to a par of wide, mahogany doors.

The driver opened his door and looked at me expectantly.

"Wait here," I said. "This probably won't take long."

He nodded, and I had Jeeves carry me up the steps to the front door where he set me down. I swung the knocker three times and waited. I heard heavy footsteps within, and the door opened revealing a large bruiser in a tan, wool suit. He had red freckles, piggy eyes, and looked like he could pick up the back end of a steam-carriage. A set of hardwood stairs rose behind him, and a hallway stretched away to the back of the house.

"What do you want?" he asked in a rumbling, gruff voice. His eyes lit upon Jeeves, but he gave no indication of caring.

"I'm here to see Mrs. O'Toole, if she's home."

"Who is it?" a woman's voice with a heavy Irish accent shouted from down the hall. She stepped around the corner. "Get out of the way, Donnie, and let me see who it is." The big man stepped aside slightly, still keeping himself between the woman and me.

There stood Mrs. O'Toole, red coif, plaid long coat, bandy legs, and all.

"Well bless my stars!" she cried. "If it isn't little Billy Patrick!" She came down the hallway towards us. She gave the big man a shove. "Go on, Donnie. Make yourself useful upstairs or something." He stepped away, gave me a suspicious look, and then lumbered up the stairs. Mrs. O'Toole smiled as she looked down at me. "Rumor had it you'd left the city or something. And here you are knocking on my door." She gave the wheelchair a once-over, and then her eyes drifted up to Jeeves. "And what on Earth is that monstrosity?"

"I guess you could call him my legs, Mrs. O'Toole." I returned the smile. "May I come inside?"

"Well, *you* certainly can, but are you sure that thing is safe?" She frowned. "I don't want my China and furniture to end up in pieces."

"Jeeves is perfectly safe. Better behaved than most adults." I smiled.

"Well, if you say so," she replied doubtfully. "It breaks it, *you* buy it."

"Yes, ma'am."

She opened the door wider and motioned for me to come in, so I did. To the left was a nicely appointed living room, with expensive furniture, a wide assortment of nick-knacks and a double-barrel shotgun over the fireplace.

"We can have some coffee in the kitchen," she said as she started walking away. "I've just brewed a fresh pot. I think your chair will fit through the hallway."

I rolled in and turned my head back. "Jeeves, come in, close door, and follow," I ordered.

The machine ducked and clumped through the doorway. As I turned I saw Mrs. O'Toole staring at Jeeves.

"Well isn't that something," she said quietly, and then disappeared into the kitchen.

"I'm sorry about your legs, Billy," she called out, sounding genuine.

"Thank you, Mrs. O'Toole." I rolled down the hallway, and my chair did make it through, but just barely. Jeeves' heavy footsteps thumped behind, so I turned into the kitchen. She had moved the chair across from her out of the way. I rolled up just she was pouring out a second cup of coffee.

"Sugar?" she asked with a smile.

I shook my head, so she moved a newspaper to the side and pushed the cup across the table. I heard Jeeves turn the corner and then stop.

Mrs. O'Toole's smile disappeared, and she gave the machine rather confused look. She shook her head and looked at me expectantly. "So, what brings you here, Billy?"

I reached into my pocket and pulled out the piece of paper. I unfolded it and slid it across the table.

Her eyes darted to the paper, half of Seamus' signature clearly visible, and then crossed her arms. The smile went flat. "I thought that might be it." The pleasantries were obviously over. "I take it this is official police business, then. Is that right, Billy?" she asked suspiciously. "I don't believe you have that authority anymore."

"I just want to find out who killed Seamus," I said flatly. "Can you tell me anything?"

"It's no secret Seamus played the numbers. Hell, half the ward plays."

"I saw him talking to you that day… just before we went to the safe house." I didn't say it as an accusation, but I saw her cheeks tighten. She knew something.

"That's right. He was placing another bet. I might even have the other half of that piece of paper lying about somewhere." Her eyes narrowed. "What of it?"

"Well, it just seems an odd coincidence, that's all. I'm trying to figure out why he's dead. Someone sold us out, Mrs. O'Toole, and Seamus, Reardon, O'Malley, and a witness ended up dead."

"Coincidence or not," she said smoothly, "I don't know anything about what happened that day. And I certainly don't know who killed Seamus or those other men." She looked me square in the eyes. She spoke evenly, without any anger, "And even if I did, I'd never spill my guts to some flatfoot or even someone who used to be a flatfoot. No offense, Billy, but you can go fuck yourself. You know how it is around here." She sounded like she was talking about the weather.

At least she was polite about it, I thought. And she was right. People in Chicago didn't talk about such things. Those who did frequently ended up in the river.

Just then a picture of a Union soldier, presumably one of her relatives, fell off the wall to my right. The glass shattered on the floor, and we both jumped. Suddenly there was a sound of rushing air and a woeful groaning, as if a man were in pain. It filled the room. We both turned our heads frantically, searching for the source, and Mrs. O'Toole's eyes went wide.

"What the Devil is that?" she hissed, terrified. Air swirled around the room, and the cupboard doors started rattling. My heart raced, and her face went stark white. The newspapers on the kitchen table fluttered violently.

"What the—" I started.

A blast of swirling air cut me off, and the newspapers flew from the table on a vortex of wind that spun around the room, carrying the newspaper pages like a flock of crazed birds. I rolled my chair backwards, my heart pounding, but I was unable to tear my eyes away from what was now happening to Mrs. O'Toole.

She made the sign of the cross and covered her head as sheets of newspaper swirled around her, pelting and slashing at her. Her exposed hands and face were covered with tiny cuts that seeped droplets and streaks of blood. She screamed again and leapt out of her chair, stumbling to her knees.

"God save us!" she cried.

I heard heavy footsteps from upstairs. Donnie had heard the commotion.

The vortex concentrated itself on her, swirling her hair and coat around as if she were in a gale. The wind roared, the cupboard doors slammed back and forth, and I could no longer hear her screams over the noise. The newspaper swirling around her came apart, tearing itself into smaller and smaller pieces like confetti.

As suddenly as it started, the wind and the slamming doors stopped.

Her screams faded, and there was nothing left but the sound of her sobbing, paper falling to the floor, and footsteps in the living room.

Just as the last shred of paper settled, a shotgun blast went off, and there was the crack of metal on metal.

I turned to see Jeeves tipping forward straight towards me, a smoking hole in its side. Its eyes flickered out, powerless. I jerked on the right wheel as it fell, but it clipped my chair, shooting me sideways to bounce off the wall and sprawl across the floor. Jeeves hit with a resounding *CLANG!*

"Maggie! Are you alright?" Donnie cried as he stepped into the kitchen. "What the hell happened in here?" he shouted.

I rolled onto my back to see Donnie standing over Jeeves, a double-barreled shotgun pointing straight at my face and a revolver stuck into his belt.

"You're a dead man," he said, glaring at me. He pulled the hammer back with a *SNICK!*

I heard a gust of wind as I shouted, "Wait! It's not what you—"

Jeeves' hand shot up faster than it had ever moved before, wrapped around the barrel, and shoved it upwards. The gun went off, and I felt a wash of heat as the slug tore through the wall above me. My ears rang. The room filled with smoke. I watched in awe as Jeeves shifted its grip to Donnie's arm.

There was a *double-CRACK* of breaking bones, and Donnie screamed as his forearm bent upwards. The big man tried frantically to pull away from the metal monster that had him in its grasp.

Jeeves lumbered to its feet, jerking Donnie left and right as it rose.

Donnie pounded at Jeeves' head, shifting it back and forth, and then he pulled the pistol from his belt. He fired into its chest, over and over again, emptying the pistol into the machine. But it didn't even slow the thing down.

Jeeves grabbed hold of Donnie's free arm. More bones cracked, and Donnie shrieked. Jeeves released Donnie's arms and wrapped its hands around the man's throat.

Donnie gurgled. His eyes popped open, and he flailed in the machine's grasp. His broken arms flopped helplessly as he struggled. His eyes bulged. His face turned red... then purple.

The flailing slowed as his eyes rolled back into his head, and finally he went limp.

The machine squeezed one final time, and a wet *CRACK* filled the kitchen when Donnie's neck broke.

Jeeves released his grip and let the lifeless body drop to the floor.

Then it turned to me, and I gasped. Its eyes burned with an eerie, unnatural blue flame that danced and flickered.

It took a step towards me with a *THUMP!*

I pushed backwards up against the wall, straining to get away from the thing.

THUMP!

"Please… don't…" I cried, but it leaned over and reached down. Its knees bent deeply putting its thighs at eye level. Then I remembered the mag-pistols.

I leaned forward and pounded on its thigh with my fist just as it placed its hands under my arms. The panel popped open, and I grabbed the pistol as it lifted me up.

"Trust…Me…Billy-Boy," it said in a familiar, albeit metallic voice.

I froze as the machine lifted me off the floor.

"Seamus?" I whispered, stupefied.

It…*he*… nodded and placed me in my chair. Without a word Seamus pointed at the floor where Mrs. O'Toole still kneeled, sobbing and shivering. And then he turned towards the window, his back to me.

I slowly rolled my chair around the kitchen table. She was curled up into a ball, and droplets of blood were already pooling beneath her slashed hands. She wept like the terrified, old woman she was.

Shreds of paper surrounded her completely, like the after-math of some bizarre parade. On the floor directly in front of her there was a clear spot. Within that spot lay four pieces of paper set in a neat row, the edges looking as if they'd been cut with scissors. Upon each piece of paper was a single, large letter.

Her sobbing slowed in the silence, and she looked up at the letters.

She gasped.

They spelled out a single word:

L I A R

She started sobbing again and tore her eyes away from the letters. She stared at me, looking as if the Devil himself had just paid her a visit.

"So, would you like to tell me what really happened that day?" I asked. "I'm no priest, but you could consider it your con-fession."

She gulped once, and her eyes turned back to the letters. Her breathing was labored as she spoke. "Your friend, Seamus," she wheezed. "He didn't just play the numbers. He played the horses too, always trying to get even. He was *way* in the red, Billy."

"How far?" I asked.

"Seven-thousand-dollars," she said weakly. I turned and looked at Seamus as he stared out the window. I suddenly real-ized that this wasn't just her confession. It was *his*. I knew what was coming.

"Bowen Nash-Davies worked for you, didn't he?" I said. "He was going to testify against you."

"Yes." She coughed and wheezed a bit more. "I gave Seamus a choice: either give up Bowen or end up in the river. It was strictly business, Billy." Her voice was almost a whisper.

"Then why kill Billy?"

"You…got there… early," she said. She was having trouble speaking.

I remembered Seamus insisting that we get coffee… and me insisting that we get going. It all fell into place.

She groaned in pain and then clutched at her chest.

"Mrs. O'Toole? Are you okay?" I asked, suddenly concerned.

"Can't… brea…." She winced, hacked out a cough, and then collapsed with her eyes wide open. Air wheezed out of her lungs in one long breath.

"Mrs. O'Toole!" *Jesus,* I thought.

"She's gone, Billy-boy," Seamus said from the window. "Heart attack… from the fear." His voice was still mechanical, but smoother now, and there was no mistaking the voice of my old friend. "The Catholics weren't right, you know. They weren't wrong either. I wish I could explain it, but there aren't words."

The reality that Seamus' ghost had taken up residence in a machine hit me like an anvil. A pang of pity took hold of me. I'd been raised Catholic, and the dead had no place amongst the living.

"You gotta move on, Seamus," I said. "Leave this place and rest."

"I can't," he said resolutely. "I still have a debt to pay. I spent my life in the red, Billy-boy. You of all people know that. I got in the red with Mrs. O'Toole. I got in the red with the Professor's brother. And I got in the red with *you*. Because I was selfish. And a coward. I figure I ought to pay at least one tab before I move on to wherever the Almighty plans to send me."

Seamus raised his arms slightly and looked down at them, slowly turning his hands and moving his fingers. The quiet hiss of pistons and whine of gears filled the room. "I'll make you a deal, Billy-boy," he said, returning his gaze out the window.

"What's that?" I asked.

"I'll give up this tin can and stop covering for your sorry ass the moment you can use your legs again or you don't need them anymore." He turned to face me. The flame around his eyes had disappeared, replaced with a bright blue glow. "Final offer. Not negotiable. And if you live a good, long life, maybe I can get out of the red just this one time."

His right eye flickered out and then came back on again. I realized he'd winked at me… just like old times.

"You drive a hard bargain," I said.

DEAD THINGS
DONT PLAY NICE

Julianne Snow

The tiny fingertips grasped the edge of the porcelain tub with all of their might, desperately trying to keep her head above water. The smooth surface was slippery but still the child strained, her knuckles turning white with exertion.

Trying a different tactic, the nails scraped at the hands that held her trapped beneath the surface. But drawing blood did not make those hands release her.

As she stared up at Mother, through the crashing waves caused by her frantic struggling, her eyes pleaded for release, for forgiveness, for anything that would stop the torment.

She knew Mother was sick. She'd even heard the doctor talking to her father when she was supposed to be playing quietly in her room. But Mother had been taking her pills and things had gotten better.

The ladies from Church barely came to visit anymore and she knew it made Mother very angry. She had seen Mother in the kitchen cursing them and promising herself she'd do something to make them notice her again.

Mother thrived on the attention she received; the pity in their eyes. It made her feel better, worthy in some odd way. The saddest part was that Mother had taken to hurting her own daughter just for the sake of that pity. First it was a broken arm, next a deep gash on her leg with a knife from the butcher's block in the kitchen. Of course it had hurt, but she never stopped loving Mother. Believing that one day Mother would show regret for the things she'd done.

Instead, it had gotten this far. It was late when Mother came into her daughter's room, the smell of alcohol strong on her breath. In the background, the rush of water echoed against the tub's walls down the hallway, the light from the open bathroom door dispelling the shadows into the far corner of her room. Mother sat down on the edge of the mattress, her hands busying themselves with different tasks like tucking her in and picking at a spot on the bed spread.

It took only a few moments for Mother to lift her up and whisk her down the hall into the bathroom. The heat of the water burned the tender skin as she was submerged, her lungs gasping for air. As hard as she fought, she was no match for the determination in Mother's eyes.

One final gulping breath of water and she lay still; the fight easing from her muscles. Looking up, she knew Mother didn't feel remorse—the big smile on her face was testament to her cruelty.

~*~

"My name is Amy, what's yours?" There was a brief pause then, "Oh, I love that name! I had an aunt with that name, but she died and I got sad."

Theresa knew what name her daughter was talking about: Mary. Her sister had played such a large role in Amy's life before her death a few months ago and from the sounds of it, a new imaginary friend had come to stay – at least for a while.

"Would you like to play with my new doll? Her name is Candy." A giggle ricocheted off the walls, only to be followed with, "I know it's a silly name, but she smells just like candy!"

Theresa went back to unpacking the boxes that lined each of the walls in their new house, content to let Amy play in her room for the time being. It was great to finally have her out from underfoot and there really was no trouble she could get into in her own room.

Theresa sighed as a small contented smile spread across her lips; the relief of the move was growing each and every day. Finally away from her abusive ex-husband, she felt that life could, and would, begin anew for her daughter and herself. There was nothing Alex could do to them since the court had decreed he'd serve time for his actions.

Listening for a moment to the giggling she heard from Amy's room, she could have sworn she heard more than one distinct cadence but dismissed it, thinking Amy was just playing up the new friend she had imagined. Theresa went back to her seemingly endless task of unpacking.

Down the hall, Amy's fascination with her new friend grew leaps and bounds.

"Why do you dress like that?" It was one of the many questions she would ask and Amy patiently waited for Mary to tell her why.

"Oh, you're going to bed? This early?" There was a pause before she said, "But I don't understand. How can you be dressed for bed in the middle of the day?"

Amy could hear her mother's voice carrying down the hall; she loved to sing and it was something the two of them did together when the radio was playing. Amy started to sing the parts of the song she knew softly to herself as Candy drank her tea with Teddy.

"What did you say, Mary?" Amy stopped singing and looked up at her new, weird friend. "Is that why you're dressed in your pajamas?" Amy listened as Mary told her why she was eternally dressed in her nightgown. Throughout the explanation, Amy said nothing. There was really nothing to say.

The story Mary shared was something Amy couldn't understand – at her young age she didn't really understand death. She just knew people went away and never came back.

When Mary pulled down the neckline of her gown to reveal the darkened welts on her chest, Amy started to cry. Not understanding what had truly happened, the tears flowed faster and harder until Theresa could hear them all the way down the hall in the bathroom.

Rushing into her daughter's room, confused and alarmed by the gut wrenching sobs, Theresa expected to find her daughter severely hurt in some way. Rounding the corner, she didn't spy any blood so at least that was a good sign.

Coming to sit at Amy's side, Theresa gathered her daughter into her arms and snuggled her securely in her lap. "Tell me what's wrong, honey," she soothed, stroking her daughter's face while gazing into her tear-filled blue eyes.

"It's Mary! Something awful happened to her!"

"What do you mean Amy? Did she go away?"

"No, Mommy, she got hurt real bad. She showed me the

marks on her chest!"

There was a keen sadness in her daughter's face at the mention of the marks so Theresa probed a little deeper. "What do you mean by marks, Amy?"

It was all a little confusing to Theresa. And the mention of marks on her body was more than a little disturbing.

"I saw them, Mommy. On her chest. Two dark spots like the kind that Daddy used to make on you before the men took him away." As Amy dissolved back into tears, Theresa held her tighter, wishing she had never been exposed to the beatings that had occurred when Alex still lived with them.

"Amy, Daddy can't hurt us anymore remember? The men who took him away locked him up for a very long time and when he gets out, he'll never be able to find us. I made sure of that." Cuddling her daughter closely, Theresa kissed the top of her head as she rocked them back and forth.

"But Mommy, I saw them. Mary was hurt by her Mommy and that's not very nice! Can we help her? Like the men helped us when Daddy was a bad man?"

The innocence in her daughter's strident face consumed Theresa and at the moment, she knew she'd do anything to help her daughter – even if it meant promising to help an imaginary friend. "Sure, sweetie, we can help Mary. She can stay with us as long as she wants and we'll keep her safe. Promise."

"Didya hear that, Mary? Mommy said that you can stay with us and that we'll protect you from your Mommy! Isn't that great? You can be like my sister!" The look of sadness wasn't fully replaced by her exuberance, but it was a start.

Theresa hugged Amy closer, glad to have figured out a way to calm her daughter.

Unbeknownst to both Amy and Theresa, Mary stood along the far wall watching the exchange, her jealousy growing with each lingering moment of the hug. Her soulless eyes bore into Theresa, her hate and vengeance channelling into a promise of intent.

~*~

Things around the new house progressed smoothly for the most part. There were more mentions of Mary and the games they played, but no more tears. Theresa counted that as a good thing. The house had been unpacked and Theresa had even started her new job as a receptionist at the local dentist's office. The pay was decent and the hours perfect as she was able to see Amy off to school and pick her up when the day was over. Life couldn't have been more idyllic and a complete one-eighty from the tumultuous time she'd spent at the hands of her ex-husband. The family had settled into a routine of sorts and it made Theresa's heart soar with joyful expectation.

However, small things had started to occur that were troubling, but it was nothing Theresa didn't think she could handle. All of the therapists she had consulted had mentioned Amy might go through a slight rebellious phase given her history, but that it would be short-lived.

It started off with Amy's toys being left in the oddest of places, like Amy was trying to see what boundaries she could push before feeling her mother buck back completely. Each instance was taken in stride, and with some careful reinforcement that toys belonged either in her room or the den which Theresa had turned into a playroom just off the kitchen, it settled down again.

Next, it was the doors. Amy was constantly leaving doors

open. Everywhere. The front door, the back door, the refrigerator door, even all of the cupboard doors. Theresa had to give it to Amy on that last one since she would have had to work out how to open the top ones without her mother hearing the chair scraping across the tiled floor of the kitchen.

Theresa found it easier to punish Amy by making her close all of the doors she had opened than by spanking her. The look she got from her daughter each time she had to close them was priceless. A look somewhere between confusion and animosity. For a brief moment, when Amy had to push the chair all the way across the floor, Theresa felt a little bit of remorse for making her shut them all, but in the end it was something she had to do.

The worst thing was that Amy blamed it all on Mary. Theresa knew that it was coming, and immediately rejected the imaginary scapegoat. There was no way an imaginary little girl was causing all of the problems. No way whatsoever. Theresa merely chocked it up to the phase and left it at that.

It was late one night, after Amy had been tucked into bed, when Theresa felt the need for a little midnight snack. The lights were off downstairs, but she still felt safe knowing the community was a good one with a low crime rate.

The accident happened while she was descending the stairs. Theresa's foot came down hard on a plastic doll and the surprise made her misjudge her footing. Tumbling to the bottom of the stairs, Theresa fought to right herself; to stop her descent before she broke something. Nothing she tried helped her and she landed in a heap.

Taking a moment to mentally take stock of her arms and legs, she swore she could hear giggling from the top of the stairs. It only took a fraction of a second for her anger to get the better of her.

"Amy! Is that you laughing up there? I could have killed myself, you stupid girl!" As Theresa gazed up into the murky shadows at the top of the stairs, she didn't see anything but she could still hear the giggles. "Amy! You'd better show yourself or else there will be hell to pay!"

Theresa screamed the last words at the top of her voice, fully expecting to hear the rapid pitter-patter of feet running away from the top of the stairs. Instead, she heard the panicked thump of two feet hitting the floor over her head and the stomping gait of her six year old coming to see what was going on.

"Mommy! MOMMY! Are you okay? Did Daddy come back? Is he hurting you? MOMMY!" The words came out in a rush, the desperation in the small voice painful to the ears.

Theresa didn't know what to think. Could her daughter have been laughing at the top of the stairs, then convincingly burst out of bed with a completely terrified and believable story?

It was implausible, but there was no other explanation.

"Mommy? Where are you? I can't see anything!"

A whimper escaped her daughter's lips but that was something Theresa would have to concern herself with later. Now she had to pick herself up off the floor before her daughter risked the treacherous climb down the stairs in the dark.

"I'm here, Amy. You stay there and Mommy will turn on the lights in a minute, okay?"

"Sure, Mommy. Is Daddy here? Did the men let him go?" The last part rose a bit more in high-pitched panic as terrible thoughts flashed through Amy's brain.

"No. Daddy is not here. Mommy just tripped on one of the toys you left lying on the stairs."

"What? I didn't leave anything on the stairs Mommy. You told me I'd get a spanking if I ever left my toys out again and trust me, I don't want a spanking."

Sometimes Theresa had to smile at the logic that came from her daughter's mouth. While she knew it was a lie, she couldn't help but shake her head at the attempt. "Amy, I don't want to discuss it at this point. I could have been killed falling down the stairs tonight – is that something you want?"

Theresa regretted the cruelty of her words as soon as she spoke them aloud. "I'm sorry sweetie," her tone softening. "I know you didn't mean to leave your toy on the stairs. I'm just upset because I fell."

"But Mommy, I didn't leave my toy on the stairs. I promise."

Theresa shakily got to her feet, grateful that nothing appeared to be broken. She'd certainly be sore in the morning, of that she had no doubt, but there would be no lasting damage. Flicking on the light, she scanned the steps, looking for the offending toy.

She found it three steps down from where she figured she'd stepped on it. There was something a little strange about it though, something Theresa couldn't readily put her finger on.

"That's not one of my toys, Mommy."

"What?"

"That's not one of my toys." Amy looked down the stairs at her mother, uncertainty clearly written across her face. "I don't have any dolls like that. You said that Barbie's were too old for me, remember?"

Theresa focussed on the toy more closely and saw it was indeed a Barbie doll. She quickly glanced up at her daughter, then back to the toy, confusion replacing the pain on her face. "I don't understand, Amy... Did you steal this from someone at school?"

"No, Mommy!"

"Are you sure? If you did, just tell me."

"No, I did not!"

Her daughter sounded more incensed than a young girl of six should, but Theresa still wasn't sure if she believed her. "I want you to go back to bed. We'll talk about this in the morning."

"But Mommy! I—"

"Go now, Amy. Before I get really angry."

The indignant stomp of Amy's feet back to her room was the only answer Theresa was going to get. Walking into the kitchen, she grabbed a glass from the dish rack and filled it with juice from the fridge. Opening the cabinet next to the sink, she grabbed the bottle of aspirin and popped off the lid. Shaking two into her hand, Theresa palmed them into her mouth and took a large swig of the orange juice from the glass. Swallowing, she looked out the window into their small backyard, wondering what she was going to do with Amy.

From the shadows, Mary watched her intently.

~*~

"Amy, I want to talk to you about what happened the other night. Would that be okay?"

Amy sat across from a dark-haired woman in an office a few days later. Theresa felt she had no other option but to seek help for her daughter. The two of them had spent the next day or so locked in a battle of wills over who had placed the toy on the stairs. Amy swore it was Mary and Theresa maintained Amy had done it.

It had gotten them nowhere and since Amy had forcefully

held her ground on the issue, Theresa knew it was time to sit down with someone more qualified at getting to the root of the problem.

"Sure." Her answer was somewhat non-committal but the doctor could handle that. Children were one of her specialties.

"Mrs. Chambers, I don't suppose you'd let me talk to Amy alone, would you?" The question wasn't out of the ordinary since children tended to open up more without their parents in the room.

"Dr. Dutta, I'm not sure—" Theresa began.

"I'm afraid I must insist, Mrs. Chambers. Amy needs to feel that what she has to say is important and that she can speak freely without getting into trouble. If she doesn't, how can I help?" The look on the doctor's face didn't allow much room for negotiation.

"Okay, I guess so. Amy, if you need me, I'll be right outside in the waiting room." Theresa squeezed her daughter's hand in a display of reassurance before standing to exit the room.

Once the door was closed, the doctor started again. "Hi, Amy. My name is Dr. Dutta but you can call me Priya, okay?"

"Okay."

"Your mother has asked me to talk to you about some of the things that have been going on in your house lately. Is there anything you'd like to share with me?"

"Not really. Mommy blames me for all kinds of stuff that Mary does, but she doesn't believe me when I tell her I didn't do it."

"Who's Mary?"

"She's my friend. When we moved in, she already lived there and Mommy said that she could stay with us and we would protect her. Mary's mommy was very mean to her and left all kinds of marks on her. Like the marks my Daddy used to leave on Mommy."

"Okay, so Mary is your friend?"

"Yes. But she gets me into trouble with Mommy so I'm not sure how good a friend she really is…" Amy let her words trail off as she stared out the window of the doctor's office.

"Have you asked Mary to stop?"

Amy's gaze returned to Dr. Dutta, a strange look taking over her face for a moment before she answered, "Of course I have. But she said it wasn't her either."

"Really? So if Mary's not doing it—"

"But Mary *is* doing it!" The child was adamant about that fact and Dr. Dutta couldn't help but be somewhat swayed by the conviction the young girl displayed.

"Can you tell me about Mary? What does she look like?"

Amy began to describe the young girl, around the same age as herself with large brown eyes, blonde hair and the marks across her body. She mentioned the long scar on the girl's right leg and the slightly odd angle of her left arm. Amy told the doctor about how she found it funny that Mary never changed out of her pajamas and how Mommy could never see her even when she was standing right in front of her.

The doctor's faced scrunched up for a moment as she wrote down what Amy was telling her, her mind racing through the different possibilities. "And what did you say about Mary's mother?"

"She was very mean to her. Mary told me her mommy was the one who broke her arm, cut her with the knife and held her under the water. It's just awful isn't it?"

As the tears flowed quietly down Amy's face, Dr. Dutta was struck again by the conviction in the way the young girl spoke. There was something she couldn't quite place her finger on, but the doubt had entered her mind. Thinking she needed to do some research, she smiled at Amy. "Is there anything else you'd like to tell me?"

"Mary says she's going to hurt Mommy." There was a pause, then Amy looked up before continuing, "How do I stop her?"

A chill ran down Dr. Dutta's spine at the softly spoken words. Did this young girl just reveal she planned on hurting her mother? Not knowing what to make of the question, she asked "What do you mean? Why does Mary want to hurt your mother?"

"Because her mommy hurt her. She says my Mommy has to pay. I don't understand why though, my Mommy never hurt Mary…"

The tears streamed in earnest now down the freckled face of the girl in front of her. Dr. Dutta had nothing to tell the girl, but tried to soothe her regardless. "Amy, Mary can't hurt your mother, okay? She's not real."

The doctor was not prepared for Amy's response.

"Then why did Mary put the Barbie on the stairs? Why did Mary open up all of the doors in the house? Why did Mary steal the knife from the kitchen?"

"Mary stole a knife, Amy?"

"Yes, from the kitchen. She took it yesterday and showed it to me. I tried to get it back, but I couldn't and I didn't want her to cut me so I stopped."

Thinking she was in well over her head with this child, Dr. Dutta paused for a moment, wondering which of her colleagues may be better suited to help the girl. "Did you tell your mother about the knife?"

"I tried, but Mommy told me not to tell stories anymore."

"Would it be okay if I mentioned it to your mother?"

"Sure. Maybe you can get her to believe you."

With her mind still reeling over the revelation, Dr. Dutta called Theresa back into the room. Once she was back inside the office, the doctor asked Amy to wait outside in the waiting room for a brief moment while she talked to her mother.

Amy got up to leave, but shot the doctor a look as she reached the door. "Please don't tell Mommy everything. Just the last thing I said was okay."

"Yes, Amy, I promise you I won't."

With one long last look, Amy left the office and Dr. Dutta closed the door behind her.

"Okay, I'm not quite sure how to say this except to say it. Amy told me that Mary stole a knife yesterday."

"Are you kidding me? That girl was never one to make up stories but ever since we moved, it's one story after another! What am I going to do?"

"For one, you're going to search your daughter's bedroom for that knife. If she has taken a knife, you need to be careful despite what you may believe about Amy. There is something going on and I would like your permission to consult a few of my colleagues about your daughter. Would that be okay?"

"Sure. I mean if you think that's the best thing to do. Do you really think she'd hurt someone?"

"I'm not certain she wouldn't, and that's what we're going to try to avoid. From my talks with you, I know that Amy spent the first few years of her life surrounded by violence. It's possible that some of that violence is bubbling back to the surface. I think you should protect yourself on the off-chance something is truly amiss with your daughter and I'll be in touch shortly when I've rounded up a few people to help me assess your daughter accurately."

Theresa's mind was reeling. Did the doctor really think Amy could do something horrible? "Thank you, Dr. Dutta. I'll be waiting for your call."

"I'll be in touch just as soon as I can. Try not to worry too much and please show your daughter all the love she's used to. A sudden change in your demeanour could certainly trigger an event none of us want."

Theresa wasn't sure what to think. Something wasn't adding up, but she planned on searching Amy's room when she got home just in case. Standing up, Theresa made it to the door before turning. "Thank you doctor. I really appreciate what you're trying to do."

"I wish you well Mrs. Chambers and I will be in touch. In the meantime, if you need anything, here's my card. I've written my cell number of the back. Do not hesitate to call me if you need anything, okay?"

"Thank you, Dr. Dutta, I will."

Exiting the office, Theresa smiled at Amy while asking her if she was ready to go. The two left hand in hand and the doctor watched from the doorway of her office. A deep feeling of foreboding washed over her, but she willed it away knowing that with the right help, Amy would be okay.

~*~

The car ride back to their small home was rather uneventful. Amy talked about nothing in particular and Theresa listened, lost in her own thoughts. Her mind kept wandering back to what Dr. Dutta had said concerning Amy and her potential for violence. While she found it hard to believe her daughter could carry such rage and malice in her tiny frame, she had once thought her ex-husband to be a kind and gentle man. Was she really that bad at reading someone's character?

"What are you thinking about, Mommy?"

"What, honey?"

"You're scrunching up your face and you only do that when you're thinking…"

"I'm sorry, sweetie, I'm just trying to figure a few things out."

"Did the lady tell you about the knife Mary stole? She said she was going to. Even asked me if it was okay for her to tell you." The earnestness in her young voice made Theresa glance to the right, lingering for a short moment on her daughter's upturned face.

"Yes, sweetie, she did. And when we get home, we're going to look for it okay?" There seemed no reason for Theresa to lie to Amy at this point. Taking another quick glance in Amy's direction, Theresa was surprised to see a look of relief on her face.

"Thank you." It was spoken so softly and so innocently that Theresa didn't quite know what to make of it. Perhaps her daughter was only acting out for attention; maybe her intentions weren't to harm anyone, especially not her own mother.

Confused yet again, Theresa said nothing, instead smiling and patting her Amy's hand reassuringly.

Once they arrived home, the two climbed the stairs and went into Amy's room. Theresa tried not to get angry at the mess of toys that littered the floor, thinking instead that cleaning up the room would make it easier to find the knife.

"What happened?"

"What do you mean, Amy?"

"My room… All of my toys are all over the floor. I had them all put away and now look at them all…"

"Maybe you forgot you played with them before we left, honey?"

"No, Mommy, I didn't have time."

There was such seriousness in her voice that Theresa didn't want to press the matter further. It was odd, that was certainly evident, but there was no other explanation.

"It's okay, honey. We'll just clean them up."

As the pair started to put away Amy's toys, Theresa felt an uneasiness set in, like someone was watching her. Every now and again she would stop and look over at her daughter who was hard at work placing each of her toys in their assigned spots, either on her bed or in the toy box.

Unable to shake the feeling, she continued cleaning while looking for the knife. When the room was put back in order, Theresa still hadn't found the knife and Amy was just as disturbed.

"Mary must have hidden it somewhere else, Mommy."

The last straw had finally fallen for Theresa. Her anger consumed her but not because she was actually mad at Amy, it had more to do with the fact she couldn't find the knife and what it would mean when Dr. Dutta heard. Theresa believed Amy had taken the knife, but didn't believe she had done so to hurt anyone. It had to have been a cry for help in some regard, a way to get her mother to give her more attention – attention Amy felt she needed. But her compassion had faded, replaced by resentment and irritation.

"Amy, stop lying to me. I know Mary is your imaginary friend and I know she is not responsible for all of the things you blame her for. So stop. Just stop. I've had enough!"

Amy stood for a moment, staring directly at her mother as the disappointment welled up in her little body. She was confused by her mother's disbelief and couldn't understand why telling the truth was getting her into trouble. "But Mommy—"

"Amy, not one more word out of you! I have absolutely had it! Now I'm done talking about this and you can stay in your room for the rest of the day. Got it?"

Her only answer was the well of tears that sprang into Amy's eyes. Feeling somewhat like a failure for losing her temper, but knowing she had to stand her ground, Theresa turned around and walked out the room, closing the door behind her.

Amy's sobs echoed from behind the door, but Theresa squared her shoulders and walked resolutely away.

~*~

Within an hour Theresa could no longer hear crying from Amy's room. Torn between checking on her to make sure she hadn't hurt herself and not wanting the histrionics to start again, she settled on taking a bath instead. A long, hot soak would certainly help to soothe her frazzled nerves.

As she turned the faucet on, Theresa swore she could hear a child whispering, but when she turned the water off again, the sound was gone. Chocking it up to her nerves and the strain she was under, Theresa decided to ignore it and turned the water back on.

Steam rose from the porcelain tub, fogging up the mirrors and relaxing Theresa just a little bit. As she stripped down to her skin, Theresa began to think about what was going on with her daughter: was there anything that had contributed to her actions of late? Could she have inherited the proclivities of her father?

Theresa eased her left foot into the hot water, then her right. Taking it slow, she slid the rest of her body into the steamy liquid scented lightly with lavender. Taking a deep breath, she closed her eyes for a moment and let the heat soothe her tired muscles.

Her hands were on each sides of the tub, helping to keep her from sliding too far down under the surface. Not realizing how much she needed to relax, Theresa started to cry, the tears freely flowing down her face. She didn't want there to be anything wrong with her Amy. She just wanted the two of them to have the opportunity to heal from the experiences of the past few years. To welcome the feeling of being safe again instead of always having to watch over their shoulders.

Wiping the tears from her face, Theresa opened her eyes and jumped when she saw the figure in the steam. It was the shape of a young girl and not believing what she was seeing, Theresa blinked to clear her vision.

When she opened them back up again, the figure was gone.

"I must be going craz—"

Theresa's head plunged below the surface, her hands desperately trying to gain purchase on the slippery edge of the tub. She came up sputtering and heard the faintest giggle from somewhere in the room. Not sure of what she was hearing, Theresa tried to stand.

Again she was forcefully plunged beneath the surface, causing her to take in huge gulps of heated water that burned her lungs. Once the pressure on her chest was released, Theresa was able to come up for air again, coughing and puking water back into the tub. She was disturbed to hear the giggling again.

"Amy, are you in here?" Theresa already knew the answer to the question before she asked it. The steam wasn't so thick that she'd be able to miss the figure of her daughter standing there in the small enclosed space. No, there was something else in the room with her.

"Mary?" Against her better judgment, Theresa gave into the name Amy had been using. "Mary, are you there?"

There was no audible answer.

Just as Theresa had made her mind up to get out of the tub again, small hands forced her back under. Kicking her feet and smacking at anything she could find with her hands did nothing but cause herself injury: a well-placed kick to the faucet had opened the skin on her toe and allowed crimson blood to stain the water and paint the tub surround in violent swatches.

Theresa fought valiantly against her unseen assailant and at times she was able to break the surface, her garbled cries for help echoing down the hallway and into Amy's room. The screams roused Amy from sleep.

The door to the bathroom burst open and Amy rushed in to see her mother being held under the water by Mary. "Stop it, Mary! Stop hurting my Mommy!"

Amy screamed at Mary and rushed to the ethereal figure beside the tub. She got her hands into the water and tried to get Mary to let go, to help lift her mother from the red-tinged depths, but an errant hit from an exhausted arm flattened her to the floor. Her face stung but she knew her Mommy hadn't meant to hurt her. Knowing Mary was too strong for her, Amy tried another tactic.

"Please Mary, don't hurt my Mommy. She loves me and she loves you. She's not like your mommy was! PLEASE!" The tears had started and the desperation in her voice was palpable.

Mary turned for a moment to look at Amy, seeing the distress on her face and smiled.

"You can't kill my Mommy just because yours killed you! That's not fair!" It was obvious to Amy that pleading with the ghost was not going to work but what else could she do? She wasn't strong enough to fight her...

Mary let a gasping Theresa back to the surface for a moment and mother and daughter shared a look. It spoke of forgiveness and belief, pain and loss, but most of all it spoke of love. Theresa knew there was nothing she would be able to do to save herself but she didn't want Amy to witness her death. It was part of the reason she had fled the abuse of her ex-husband. But somehow she had wandered unknowingly into an even more dangerous situation.

Mary forced her back under the surface again as Amy cried from the tiled floor. Theresa continued to fight until her body couldn't take it any longer. When all was still, Mary released Amy's mother and disappeared into the air.

~*~

It was two days later when the police broke into the home Theresa Chambers shared with her daughter Amy. After being alerted by Dr. Dutta for the unanswered calls, it was decided someone should take a look through the house.

They were unprepared for what they found.

In the upstairs bathroom they found the body of Theresa Chambers, in the foul, blood stained tub with two dark bruises on either side of her mottled chest. On the floor, they found Amy, sitting with legs crossed, rocking back and forth. She was covered in blood and crying to herself softly about Mary.

Unable to answer questions when asked, she was transferred to the local psychiatric hospital under the care of Dr. Priya Dutta. Subsequent assessment and questioning revealed Amy has undergone a few changes. In fact, Mary is always with her now and only comes out to play when challenged. And trust me; she doesn't like being challenged…

CALLIOPE

Jess Russell

You speak of my love like
You have experienced love like mine before

But this is not allowed
You're uninvited
An unfortunate slight

Uninvited ~ Alanis Morissette

Preface

I stared out my bedroom window admiring the thick blanket of white snow falling onto the peaks of grass below. The hole in my chest had grown triple in size over the past month. The hollowness pulled me inward and imploded over and over again. Every breath I took felt like I had swallowed a box of razor blades and allowed them to cut me from the inside out. It was pure torture.

But it wasn't because she was gone. It was because no one believed that she was still here...

I could feel her.

"I'm so sorry for your loss, Jimmy." The words were on repeat everywhere I went. It was like going on the "It's a Small World" ride at Disney World over and over again. I knew every time I'd leave the house, everyone I'd see would say it, and their words would once again tug at the already enormous hole in my heart. Their expressions were all the same; full of pity and sympathy, and sometimes, curiosity. None of them knew there was nothing to feel sorry for and I couldn't explain it to them.

When I tried to tell my sister, she looked at me with sad eyes and frowned, "It feels that way sometimes, doesn't it?" she said.

"It feels that way all the time," I argued. "She's still here, Penny. Can't you feel her?" I pleaded. I needed her to understand and believe that I *wasn't* going crazy, but she couldn't. No one could. She simply patted me on the shoulder with a frown and left the room. I felt so defeated.

Her soul was everywhere I looked. Bright waves of light floated around me, or outside in the dark of night her light would shine through my window, comforting me as I wept. It was like staring at the Northern Lights in the middle of December just outside my bedroom. She felt my presence and I felt hers. And I could tell she was struggling. She was in dire need of finding a new home. A new temporary vessel for her soul to take on so we could be together again.

But when I woke up that late February morning, she was gone. No bright lights, no waves of warmth, no feelings of calmness or serenity.

My Calliope was gone.

I searched the house up and down. I ran out into the streets frantically searching for her light. The fear inside consumed me, wondering and worrying that I had indeed just gone crazy and imagined the radiant rays of light that surrounded me every day. But when the sun beat down on the snow before me, showing its sparkling diamond glisten, I knew.

I stood in the middle of the street, panting and shaking and sweating, bent over at the waist with my hands on my knees, but I knew.

Calliope had found a new vessel.

~*~

Part One

I stood on the corner of Main Street and Commercial, trying to feel what direction to take. Her light was gone, but I could feel her energy. It was like a magnet. I started to go right, but her energy died inside of me, so I turned around and went left.

I walked down the block and watched as the small shops turned their open signs over to let everyone know the day had finally begun. I continued walking in the direction I was being pulled, but my insides felt weak. My head spun out of control and my eyes couldn't focus.

Calliope was struggling.

She couldn't handle being inside the new body. I could feel everything she was going through. The want and need to hold on for as long as possible radiated through me, but her fingers were slipping.

I steadied myself and forced my legs to keep going. I was

headed in the right direction.

I came to an intersection and the flashing red "Don't Walk" sign blinked at me derisively from the other side. The early morning rush hour had started so when I looked both ways down the road, I knew I'd have to wait. Her pull tugged at me hard.

Patience, I thought. I shook my head with a small smile forming on my lips. She was always in a hurry to go nowhere. Tugging on my arm, running around the house frantically searching for her keys and coat and shoes, afraid of being late. We were that annoying couple who always showed up fifteen minutes early to everything. But I didn't care. I just smiled and nodded because she was so adorable when she was stressed, and I loved her that much.

I'd wait with her for hours or days or weeks on end, as long as we were together.

I looked up at the light that still hadn't changed. I absent-mindedly observed the world around me, watching my breath each time I exhaled into the cold morning air. I stepped away from the curb as a car drove past, splashing dirty slush onto my feet. I leaned against the light pole and pressed the crosswalk button again and found my eyes wandering to an old ragged man on the other side of the street. He wore a long, brown, dirty trench coat and his head shook back and forth as he paced in the alley way in between two buildings. His lips twitched and jumbled sounds echoed through the air, but his words were incomprehensible. I felt the pull inside of me get stronger.

Finally, the man made of light that signaled it was safe to cross appeared on the sign, and I sprinted to the other side. I turned left around the pole and approached the babbling man.

I stood a few feet away from him and listened as he

muttered incoherently to himself. He hadn't noticed me yet. I cocked my head to the side and furrowed my brows, trying to understand what he was saying. I took two steps closer.

"I told her, I said you can't do that but no, she wouldn't listen to me, no, no, no, I'm always wrong and she's always right, and look what happened now, just look at her," the man barked to no one. I stopped two feet in front of him as he continued to pace before me.

I cleared my throat. "Excuse me?"

He didn't look up. He continued walking back and forth muttering things to himself about a woman he'd known, or maybe only imagined, I couldn't tell.

"Excuse me, Sir?" I asked again.

He glanced at me for a moment, but quickly turned away. I was of no interest to him. I growled in frustration, wondering why I felt so compelled to speak to this man. I tried to turn around and walk away, but a sharp pain in my stomach jolted me to a stop. I turned back.

Calliope was telling me to stay.

The man, who I was pretty sure was schizophrenic, continued muttering to himself completely unaware of my existence. I eyed him warily for a moment longer, contemplating turning around again because I had no idea how to get this man's attention, how to pull him out of his crazed trance. But at that moment, another strong jab caused me to lurch forward, and I fell at his feet. I grabbed hold of myself and leaned up against the building to my right.

She was pulling me.

My eyes widened and my jaw trembled. I looked up to the man again and said the only thing I could think to say, "Calliope!"

My hand reflexively reached out to him as I said it, with the other holding onto my chest. The man stopped dead in his tracks and slowly turned around to meet my gaze. His eyes popped wide as they bore into mine. He jumped towards me, wildly, shaking his head, ""Yes! Yes! She's the one! I told her no, but she wouldn't listen! She did it anyway! But it won't work! It's against the rules! She can't stay!" he screamed in my face. His body twitched strangely as he spoke. His head jerked to the side and his hands flinched anxiously.

I pushed myself away from the building. "You know her? Please! I have to find her! Do you know where she is?"

He shook his head, "No, no, no, she's gone now. She took her. She took my Bonnie! But she won't last, it won't work, she can't stay, no no no. It doesn't work like that!"

"What doesn't work? Who did she take?"

He moved away from me and began pacing the alley way again. "No, no, no, she can't do that … She can't stay in there, she has to leave! They won't let her stay! It's against the rules! But she wouldn't listen to me, no, no, no."

I shook my head and pulled on his arm, "Where did she go?!"

He eyed me, almost terrified. "She left... Not here anymore, no, no, no. Gone with my Bonnie... She took my Bonnie!" Tears began to swell in the poor old man's eyes and I let him go. He moved back against the wall of the apartment building and slunk down. His words became whispers and I knew he couldn't be any more help to me.

I reached inside my pocket and pulled out all the money I had. I wasn't sure if he even knew what it was or how to use it, but I set it down at his feet anyway, hoping he would understand my gratitude.

I turned around and went back down the road, contemplating the man's words. He had seen Calliope and she had taken his Bonnie. Calliope must have taken this Bonnie woman's body as a new vessel, but she couldn't keep it. But why? Why would she have to leave? And how did this man know all of this? Was he psychic? Clairvoyant? Or was he really just a crazy old man who talked to himself?

No, he was much more than that, he had to be. He knew too much, things that he shouldn't have known. He was definitely not crazy. Thinking over the situation made me wonder... what if mentally ill people really weren't ill at all? Maybe they were just in touch with worlds the rest of us couldn't even imagine, and therefore can't understand?

I shook the thought out of my head and continued my way down the block. The pull of her energy grew stronger, yet weaker at the same time. I could sense her struggle, I just couldn't understand why. What was making her fight so hard to stay?

A sharp jolt in my stomach caused me to instinctively turn around. Across the street, I recognized Haven Park and in the middle stood a large fountain surrounded by a circular concrete walkway. Standing in front was an old battered woman, staring at me. Relief filled my insides. Warmness took over my body as the blood flowed faster through my veins. I felt every heartbeat in my chest grow stronger with each breath I took.

Calliope.

I ran to her, calling out her name, dodging the cars as I crossed the busy street. Her eyes didn't move, nor did they blink. She was frozen. I wasn't sure if she could see me, but I knew she felt me. Because I could feel her. Her energy was calling to me, pulling me in like a fish on a reel. And right as I stepped up onto the curb, it happened.

Her eyes snapped shut and she gasped.

I was only a few feet away when I watched her collapse. Her body stiffened before it began to writhe uncontrollably.

"No!" I screamed.

A man on a bench jumped up and ran to her side. He knelt down in attempt to help, taking hold of her head to prevent it from being hit against the concrete.

"Someone call 911! She's having a seizure!" he shouted. A crowd of onlookers surrounded the scene. Curiosity always got the best of people. No one had any idea what was really happening, and neither would a paramedic.

But only because no one else could see it.

Calliope was fighting. I watched as she struggled with the soul already inside the woman's body. She was trying to push Calliope out. The lights came from the woman thrashing on the hard, cold ground. Two beams of white light going in and out, back and forth, fighting for control. My insides ached. The desperation she felt flowed through my body like an electric shock.

Calliope was losing.

Then the lights collided into each other, bright and loud, and it was over.

The woman stopped convulsing and her light disappeared. Gut wrenching anguish flowed through my veins as I watched the woman lay lifeless. Neither soul had won and she was left empty.

~*~

Part Two

I turned and walked away from the crowd. My head hung low and my arms dangled weakly at my sides. Every ounce of strength I had in me was ripped out in one fell swoop. Tears ran down my cheeks. Devastation consumed me whole.

I was so close.

We were so close.

I closed my eyes and tried pushing away the horrible feelings so I could find Calliope. I focused everything I had... but her pull was gone. The energy dissipated when she collided into the other soul. I could no longer feel the gravity drawing me to her. I looked around trying to find her light floating somewhere nearby, but it wasn't there.

I panicked.

My entire body ached painfully. The lump in my throat turned into a massive ball that stretched outward, pushing against my organs. I stumbled clumsily into a mailbox to hold myself up, but it hurt to breathe.

My chest grew tighter and tighter with each breath I took. My vision became blurred and disorientated. What was happening to me?

What was happening to us?

I felt a warm touch on my back and a concerned voice speak, but the words were muffled. I closed my eyes and slipped off the mailbox, falling hard onto my back. The sky was gray and dismal, and I was spinning out of control. The clouds began moving too quickly, it made me dizzy. My body was sinking deeper and deeper into blackness, the earth itself was consuming me whole. I could feel it crack underneath my body and slowly pull me under...

A blurred face appeared above me, moving in circles. I

blinked numerous times, and very slowly, it came into focus.

"Jimmy! Breathe, man!" he cried. I felt his hands touch my face and slap my cheek. I blinked again and his face became clear. Recognition clicked in my head.

"Colin?"

He sighed in relief, "Are you alright, man?"

I sat up from the cold ground and nodded. "Yeah, I think so... I don't know what happened," I lied.

"You stopped breathing," he explained.

I couldn't breathe, I thought. He took my hand and helped me to my feet. I brushed the snow off my coat while Colin helped. He eyed me concerned, "You sure you're okay?"

I kept my eyes on my feet as I breathed in deeply and like a swift kick to the gut, her essence surrounded my body, filled my lungs with relief, joy and calmness. The worry that I had lost her was gone, and she was back.

I looked at him, "I am now. Thanks, Colin."

He nodded and gave me a half smile. "No problem. So, how have you been? I haven't seen you since—" He stopped in mid-sentence.

"It's alright. You can say it. Since the funeral," I finished for him.

He ran his fingers through his hair and smiled awkwardly, "Right, sorry. Your sister said you were having a hard time, so I didn't want to bother you..."

"Penny worries too much. I'm fine," I cut him off and shot him a weak smile.

I started walking down the street again, waiting for Calliope to guide me in the right direction.

"So, what have you been up to?" Collin asked as he followed, glancing at me every so often with a worried expression. "I haven't seen you at work. Did you take a leave of absence?"

"Yeah," I said. "Something like that."

Colin nodded. "Still staying with Penny?"

"For now." I knew he just was trying to catch up with me, but in all honesty, I wasn't in the mood. I hadn't really spoken to anyone but my sister since Calliope's funeral, and I'd barely left the house. The only reason I went anywhere was because Penny begged me to, and I needed my sister to see that I was fine, even though it was a lie. Today, however, I had left on my own agenda and wouldn't go back until I was finished.

I looked around the block, searching for any sign of Calliope. Colin eyed me curiously, "Are you looking for something?"

I turned to face him with uncertainty, "Um... No, I just thought I saw someone..." My voice faded when something behind him caught my eye. A few yards away, a long stream of light floated in and out of a large crowd walking across the intersection. My eyes popped wide and my breathing increased. "I have to go, Colin. It was nice seeing you," I said, and ran.

I heard him call out my name from behind, but I ignored him. Her light pushed through the crowd, in and out of people, trying to take control. I watched her jump from person to person quicker than I had ever seen anything move in my life. After trying everyone in the crowd, she moved to the sidewalk on the other side of the street, working her way up the road. She bounced impatiently off each person, some of whom barely notice her futile attempts, while others came to abrupt stops until she was pushed out. Confusion took them over before they regained themselves and continued on their way.

She reached the end of the road where an old lady with a

cane was getting into a cab. Right as the woman pulled her cane in, Calliope's light entered her chest, and didn't come out. I sprinted even faster, calling her name. The woman stared ahead blankly, unsure what was happening. The driver closed her door for her and ran back around to the driver's side.

I screamed, "CALLIOPE!"

But it was useless. Before I could get close enough, the taxi had pulled away from the curb with her still inside.

Out of breath and frustrated more than ever, I rammed my foot into the street sign. My hands dug into my hips painfully as I paced the corner, physically and mentally exhausted. I didn't know how much more I could take. My efforts seemed useless. Why was it that every time I got closer, she was ripped away from me again? It wasn't fair. I needed her. My life meant nothing without her.

I watched the taxi turn around a corner, and she was gone. Feeling completely helpless, I fell onto a bench and my head fell into my hands. I pulled hard on my hair and growled. Where was she going? Why didn't she tell the driver to turn around so she could get out? I pushed myself back to my feet wondering what the hell I was going to do, when a sharp pain jabbed at my chest. I let out a cry and wrapped my arms around myself. Someone had reached inside my body and tried ripping my heart out. Anger and impatience flowed through me now, and I knew it was her.

Calliope was mad... She was mad at me because I didn't follow her.

I smiled meekly when I realized she hadn't given up yet. And I couldn't either.

I followed my gut. I made my way across the street, following where the taxi had taken her. I didn't have a clue to where

I was going, but I trusted my instincts and knew she would guide me in the right direction.

I walked for blocks. Staring straight into nothing, my mind wandered. Everything surrounding me ceased to exist, until finally, I fell before a bright red sign, buzzing in my mind. The fuzzy words came in and out of focus and I was finally able to read them.

OPEN.

Relief grew within me as I approached the automatic doors of the supermarket and stumbled inside.

~*~

Part Three

I stood in front of the meat freezer, where dozens of frozen chickens lay wrapped in white and yellow plastic with metal hooks nailed into to the bones of their legs. On the shelves behind them were a mixture of sauces I assumed were used as marinade. Any other day, this picture would have made my stomach sick, not having eaten meat since I was a teenager. But at that moment, I couldn't see them for what they were; poor, defenseless, innocent animals that were slaughtered by the hands of some ignorant butcher with absolutely no compassion for life, one who enjoyed killing far too much.

Normally, that is exactly what I would have seen, but now... I couldn't see anything.

My mind was in a fog. I wanted to move and make this wretched feeling go away. I needed to move. It was so cold with the air from the freezer blowing on my face, but my feet were glued to the floor.

Another dizzy spell took over and I closed my eyes, hoping it would pass. I took a few deep breaths and let my hands fall onto the cold metal side of the freezer. I opened my eyes and let out a long breath.

Why is she keeping me here? I thought.

"You won't find her here," said a small voice from behind, startling me. I glanced over my shoulder to see a small girl with bright blonde hair that hung down to her back, and piercing blue eyes that bore into mine. She wore a light blue polka dot dress with a white sweater over her shoulders. Her Mary Jane shoes tapped against the floor as she came closer. "She's already gone."

I quirked an eyebrow at her, "Excuse me?" I asked.

"I said she's gone."

"Who?"

She smiled. "Calliope, of course."

My heart skipped a beat. "You know Calliope?"

She nodded. "You just missed her," she explained as she skipped past me, and headed down the aisle behind us.

I lifted my feet from where I stood and smiled when they finally did as they were told. I followed the girl down the aisle, watching her scrutinize the shelves with care. "When was she here? How do you know it was her?" I asked.

The girl turned around, flashing her brilliantly white smile. "About ten minutes ago. And I always know when they're here, silly. It's my job," she laughed and continued down the aisle, examining the cookies.

I furrowed my eyebrows, "Your job?"

"Mhmm," she said as she picked up a package, frowned, then placed it back on the shelf.

"What exactly is your job?" I asked.

"To find them."

"Find *who*?"

She turned and looked at me significantly, "The lost ones. It's my job to help them find their way home."

She turned back to the cookies again and picked up a dark brown bag, turning it in different angles, scrutinizing it carefully. She shook her head and put it back. She looked up at me questioningly, "Jimmy, would you mind helping me? I'm looking for my father's favorite kind of chocolate chip cookies and can't seem to find them."

I startled when she said my name, "You know who I am?"

"Of course I do!" she exclaimed and rolled her eyes.

I nodded, confused, but turned to the selection before me. I don't think I had ever seen so many different kinds of chocolate chip cookies in my life. "Um... do you know what they look like?" I asked her.

She nodded, "Oh yes, they have a big yellow flower on the front, with a blue sky behind it. They really are quite good."

I searched the shelves high and low and saw no such packaging. I shook my head, "I don't see anything. Are you sure that's right?"

"Oh yes, I'm sure. Daddy buys them here every time we visit."

I continued to look for the correct package but wasn't having any luck, and to be honest, I didn't have the patience for it either. I sighed anxiously, "Look, little girl, I really appreciate your help, but I don't have time for all this. I need to find Calliope."

She turned and smiled at me, "Oh, don't worry. You have time. She's the one who brought you here, didn't she?"

A twinge of eeriness and suspicion pulled at my stomach. "How do you know all this?" I whispered.

"I already told you, it's my job," she answered.

I blinked and took a deep breath, "You said it's your job to help lost ones find their way home."

"Yes, but I have many jobs, Jimmy. And I know more than you could possibly imagine."

I shook my head and pinched the bridge of my nose. "If you know so much, then you have to know where she went. Please, I need to find her. Did you help her find her way home?"

The girl frowned and shook her head, "No, she got away before I had the chance," she started, and I let out a breath of relief. She met my gaze and took hold of my hand, comfortingly. "I know why she ran away from me, Jimmy. She's looking for you. She's not ready to let you go." Her tone was soft and sad, almost empathetic.

I squeezed her hand, "Can you help me find her?"

She looked at me sorrowfully, "Oh, I'm not supposed to. I could get into a lot of trouble..."

"Please... I need to find her... Please..." I begged as I fell to my knees.

I had felt Calliope's presence around me ever since the accident, I couldn't give up now. I couldn't let her go when I was so close to getting her back.

The little girl's eyes filled with sympathy and she placed her warm, tiny hand on my face. Her thumb brushed away a tear that had escaped my eye, and warmth rushed over me, that for the first time in months, calmed my nerves. She let out a deep breath, "You need to understand, Jimmy. There are rules, and Calliope broke them. I don't know how she got away with it... But she won't last much longer. A new vessel can't keep her for very long."

I shook my head, confused, "Why?"

"Because it's against the rules. If a spirit were allowed to enter a new body whenever they wanted to, the world would be a mess. It would be filled with confusion, and a lot of lost people. A soul is only allowed to enter a body that's not their own when that body is in need of repair, or when the original soul is too broken to fix itself. It's not something easily done. It takes a lot of strength to stay in an unfamiliar body. When I saw Calliope's light inside of that nice old lady, I knew she was stronger than any soul I've ever seen before. Her love for you is so strong, Jimmy. But she can't stay. It's her time."

I stared at the little girl, who could be no more than ten, completely marveled. I didn't think it was possible for a child to know all of this. How someone so young and inexperienced could possibly have these answers, but I was wrong. Adults take children for granted, never listening to what they have to say, never appreciating the way their minds work, when in reality, a child's mind is the most brilliant of them all. It's not convoluted or polluted by hate and invented judgment of people and the world around us.

In that moment, I realized that all the answers we seek within the universe lie within the innocence of children.

Another stray tear fell down my cheek. "Is there a way she can stay longer without growing weaker? Just long enough for me to say goodbye?"

She looked around the aisle nervously before slowly moving her lips to my ear. She whispered soft, quiet words that rang through my mind with instant revelation.

I knew where to find Calliope.

I wrapped my arms around the little girl and cried into her shoulder. She patted my back comfortingly before pushing herself up to meet my gaze.

"Thank you," I whispered, and turned to make my way out of the store.

~*~

Part Four

A buzzing from my coat pocket startled me. I pulled out my cell phone and saw the name "Penny" flash repeatedly in a blue light. I didn't answer. The message box on my phone informed me that I had eight missed calls, two new voice mails, and twelve unread text messages. It buzzed in my hand again, and I answered in defeat.

"Hello?" I said as I quickened my pace down the street.

"Jimmy?! *Where are you*?! Are you okay?!"

"I'm fine, Penny. I just... I had to get out of the house."

"You haven't left the house in a month! What is going on?!"

"Nothing, I just had a few errands to run," I said hoping to calm her nerves. It didn't work.

"At six o'clock in the morning?! Jimmy, please come home. The kids just got on the bus for school, I made some coffee. Come home, and we can talk."

I pulled the phone away from my ear and checked the time. I hadn't realized how long I had been gone. It was already quarter past eight.

"I can't come home right now, Penny. I have something I

need to do."

"Jimmy, please. You shouldn't be alone right now. How about I meet you for breakfast? Tell me where you are."

"No, I can't right now."

"Well, what are you doing? I'll come with you. I'll help," she insisted.

"Penny, please, you can't come with me."

"Why not? I'm worried about you, Jimmy. Won't you at least tell me where you're going?"

I paused for a moment, listening to her breath on the other end of the line. Penny knew where I was going, or at least she was afraid she knew. Penny didn't want to believe that I could see Calliope, that I could feel her essence around me every minute of the day. She didn't want to think that her big brother had gone mad over the death of his wife.

"Penny," I started on the verge of tears, "I'm so close, I can feel her... She's here ... She's waiting for me."

I heard a long hard sigh on the other end of the phone, "I know how hard this is for you, Jimmy. Calliope loved you more than I have ever seen another person love before. She was so good to you, and what happened was tragic, but you need to let her go. She's gone, and I'm sorry, Jimmy, but she's not coming back."

I heard her choke back tears as she spoke. I closed my eyes and tried to swallow the massive lump in my throat. "She's not gone, Penny. I know you don't understand, but I *know* how to find her now. Please, just let me..." I begged.

"Jimmy, come home, and we'll call Dr. Harper. Maybe she can give you something to help..."

But before Penny could finish, I pulled the phone away from my ear and snapped it shut.

I took out my bus pass and stepped outside, just in time for the 8:35 into the city. The gravitational pull I felt was stronger.

As I sat down on the bus, I looked out the window and smiled widely as the beams of sunlight hit my face because I knew I was headed in the right direction.

An hour later the bus came to a stop in front of a group of odd buildings I was especially familiar with. Calliope and I would come here often to visit him. He was a nice old man who truly loved his granddaughter. He'd taken her in as a teenager after her mother died, and raised her as his own. Even after he'd become unable to take care of himself, he always knew how to take care of Calliope. She would ask his advice and he always seemed to know what to do, even if his answers didn't make sense at the time. Grandpa had been diagnosed with dementia two years ago and the doctors told us he would never recover.

Only now did I understand that it was not his mind he had lost.

The last time Calliope and I came to visit was four days before the accident. As I stepped off the bus, the guilt of not coming back to see him after she had passed cut into me deeply. He deserved better than that.

I approached the nursing homes double doors and went inside. The nurse at the front desk smiled, "Hello, Mr. Noble! How are you doing today?" She asked.

I simply smiled and nodded.

"No Mrs. Noble?"

My face fell and I shook my head, "No, not today. Calliope... isn't feeling like herself."

"Oh, I'm sorry to hear that. Give her my best, will you?"

Instead of feeling hurt that the nurse remained oblivious to that fact that my wife had died, I simply smiled, "I'll tell her when I see her."

She handed me a visitor's pass, "Mr. Griffin is in the lounge right now, but I should warn you, he's been feeling a little off today. Having a hard time keeping his mind straight, you see. It's good that you came, though. He's been asking for you." My heart fluttered. I could feel the tears swell up in my eyes as I thanked her and made my way to the lounge.

The lounge was filled with other residents and caretakers, watching television or playing various board games. I observed them quietly as I passed. Everything went by in slow motion, and my head was swimming in a sea of jumbled thoughts and muffled whispers, until finally, everything became still and silent. It was like time itself had stopped, and I was being pulled by some external force into an alternate universe.

A flickering of light caught my attention, and a strange vision stood before me, standing at the open lancet windows with the sun shining directly on its face. At first, her grandfather stood before me, old and hunched over. But a blur of another being passed in front of me, and suddenly, Calliope was standing in his place, young and bright and perfect. Her long brown hair blowing gracefully in a breeze, her bronze skin radiating in the sunlight. Her eyes were closed and she tilted her head toward the sun, allowing it to warm her face.

"Calliope?"

She opened her eyes and turned to me with a smile. "Jimmy," she whispered. Tears swelled in my eyes as I approached her slowly. "I knew you would find me."

I smiled back. "I knew you wouldn't give up until I did."

She nodded. "That is true." She held her hand out to me

and I took it, grateful and joyful and surprised at how real it felt. It didn't feel like the wrinkly, thinning skin of an old man. It felt warm and strong and as soft as silk.

Calliope pulled me to sit with her on a small couch behind us. I sat next her, staring at her marveled and amazed and grateful to the universe for giving me another chance to be with her again. She was my other half, my soul mate, my whole reason for being.

"I've missed the sun," she said.

I smiled, "No, Calli. The sun has missed you." I traced my thumb on the back of her hand in circles. She looked down at our hands intertwined together and back up to meet my face.

"I can't stay much longer, Jimmy."

My heart sank at her words and the pain crept back up my throat. "I know," I swallowed hard, pushing the bile down. "But I couldn't let you leave without saying goodbye. Or without telling you how much I love you, and how sorry I am..." I choked.

"His soul was so lost and broken. It was the only reason I could get inside his body."

"And because he's your family. There's a connection to you that made it familiar. It helps the soul be comfortable there. It's not as foreign."

Calliope smiled. "She told you, didn't she?"

I nodded.

"I knew she would. She is a nice girl, always helping people. She let me go, you know. She wasn't supposed to but she felt it, too; the energy between us. Said she'd never felt anything like it before."

I looked at Calliope longingly. "How long do you have?"

"Not long. Grandpa's body is old and can't keep me much longer. It's his time too." I looked down and squeezed her hand hard. "Don't be sad, Jimmy. It will be okay. You can go on without me. You're supposed to."

I couldn't be sure about that. It hurt too much. It was too hard. My chest was caving into my body, slowly and painfully, breaking my ribs and shoving the jagged edges into my organs. I needed her. Calliope was like air; without her, I couldn't breathe.

She lifted her hand to my face and caressed it softly. "Jimmy," she whispered. A single tear rolled down my face and she wiped it away. "I love you. Forever."

"Calli... Don't go... Not yet, please."

"I've broken so many rules..."

"It's because we're special. We're connected."

She nodded. "But this isn't the end, Jimmy. We'll be together again."

"In another life?" I asked.

"In another life," Calliope answered.

I could see her fading now, her light glowing dimmer at each passing second and I felt my body crumble. I wept uncontrollably as I squeezed her hand as tight as I could, trying to keep her with me for as long as possible. "NO! You can't leave me now! Not yet! I won't let you go!" Calliope turned her body so it faced mine and put her free hand on my face. It was so warm against my cheek. Closing my eyes, I pressed myself into her. "I don't know how to live this life without you..."

"You will," she breathed. "I've seen it."

My eyes shot open and locked with hers. Her pull was stronger than ever and instantly, I felt my body fill with the calm I'd been craving for so long. Light and air and tranquility flooded my veins and spilled over my insides, washing away the fear and sadness and anger. The desperate desire I'd been feeling for so long was gone, and was replaced with gentle, quiet contentment. Calliope had finally given me the peace I needed as she looked into my eyes one last time before her light faded completely.

"I love you."

And she was gone. All that was left before me was the lifeless body of an old man, whose hand rested peacefully in mine. His head lay on the back of the sofa, his eyes closed, his spirit soaring.

Calliope showed me my future without giving away how my story would end. Everything made sense now. Nothing was clouded or foggy like it was before, but as clear as the blue sky on a summer day. I knew where I belonged now. I knew what needed to be done.

I stood up from the sofa, still holding Grandpa Griffin's hand in mine, and placed a gentle kiss on his forehead. "Goodbye, my love. And to you too, Grandpa." I called out for the nurses, who ran in the room frantically, checking for a pulse that I knew wasn't there. I let his hand drop from mine as I turned and left the room.

~*~

Everything is still now. My life is filled with a calmness I never imagined I'd have again. Her face has faded, but still lingers on. I see her in my mind sometimes, and I know she is all right.

And so am I.

LORALEE AND THE GREEN

Chrissy Moon

I was having so much fun at school that I almost forgot how much I loved holding lighters under animals' heads.

We were not allowed to have lighters. Of course. And at thirteen years old, I had ZERO interest in smoking. Okay, I had a *little* interest, but we couldn't light up anyway, so what was the point? In the days before my parents shipped me off, I used to steal my dad's lighter pretty often. The lure of a small creature gasping painfully as it burnt to a crisp was just too powerful.

Not too long after there was an unfortunate event involving Sheila Branson's pet turtle, I was taken to this New York boarding school.

Coincidence?

Actually, it was. I was a little off, but I had one of the highest IQs in my small town. Wittenkey was an elite school for the intellectually gifted, and I was always at the top of my class, having skipped two grades a couple years ago.

I loved Wittenkey. It was an *awesome* place! We had our own rooms and didn't have to share with *anybody*. We were like superstar kids.

You're my new diary, so I'll tell you about myself. My name is Loralee. Isn't that the prettiest name you've ever heard? I have always loved it. I don't mean to brag, but besides being the smartest girl in school, I was also the most popular. I ruled the halls.

On this day, however, the halls were quite different. They were darker than they usually were. The modern sconces on the wall didn't shine as bright. There were more patches of pitch-black shadow, and they seemed to be everywhere that I looked.

Eventually I looked up and realized I'd been paying so much attention to the halls that the crowd I was more or less walking with had wandered off. Everyone was probably in the dining hall by now. But there wasn't any time to think about that because every step I took had a slight echo, and it was unnerving.

I looked straight ahead as I walked, but out of the corner of my eye I saw a shadow move along the wall.

Behind me and to the right.

I stopped in my tracks. So did the shadow. I continued walking.

And so did the shadow.

Maybe it was my own silhouette? There was only one way to find out. I lifted my right hand to scratch my nose.

There was no such corresponding movement in the shadow.

And it was still following me.

I didn't have to actually turn around and look behind me to know that it was a vile monster-ghost that I simply called The Green. It was always chasing me and taunting me, whispering horrid threats in my ear, telling me what terrible things it wanted to do to me.

And then, once a week, it walked right through the walls of my dorm room and left me in bruises.

I realize now that it had been this way ever since I got to this school. I don't know why I kept remembering and forgetting, but I was determined now to always be aware of this terror. Maybe it was just because I wanted to pretend that everything was just fine, and most of the time, it really was.

No one else at school knew what The Green even was, so I didn't really open up to anyone else about it. It was just attacked *me*. It just hated *me*.

Did it hate me because of my problem with fire? Was it because of that cat I'd stabbed through the chest when I was younger? I hadn't tortured or killed any animals since I'd been at Wittenkey. I'd confessed to these sins in church but still dreamed of killing things. I didn't know why. I couldn't help it. I told Father Neil that I still had these urges that kept me awake at night.

That, and my fear of The Green.

In the hallway, I was panicking but I was trying desperately not to show how afraid I was. I just walked faster, and it was impossible *not* to notice that the shadow was also moving faster along the wall.

I wasn't even trying to get to the dining hall anymore – I just wanted to outrun The Green and get to safety. Was it possible to outrun a monster-ghost? Deep down inside, I knew it wasn't. But I kept walking fast, which eventually turned into a full-fledged run.

I couldn't afford extra breath to sob with, even though I wanted to do that very much. I just kept running, stumbling and fleeing from The Green, that *thing* that was creating that shadow. I kept running away from the fear.

I rounded the corner. I was now in a small wing that led to the school garden. But I almost wanted to give up. I was *so* scared. Goose bumps popped up all over, making me almost feel like my skin was shrinking.

Then I heard it. Shoes slapping on the tile right behind me. Rapidly.

Why would a monster-ghost wear shoes?

And then I heard something else, and my insides ran cold.

It was a laugh. For some reason I think anytime I heard The Green's voice, it had sounded different. This time, the laugh was feminine, but to me it sounded like it was saying, *I am enjoying chasing you. I am amused, not worried. I know I'm about to catch you, and I will bring Hell and force-feed it to you.*

I was not yet at the garden door, and it didn't seem like I was going to make it there. Fully expecting to be killed any moment now by an insane monster-ghost, I flung open the nearest door, hoping it would be unlocked and that I could stay inside until The Green had passed me by.

I slammed the door behind me and turned around.

Surprise, surprise! I was in the dining hall.

I breathed deeply for a few seconds and felt my heartbeat slow back down to normal.

How did I end up here? Had I been running here without really thinking about it? Well, all the better, I supposed. Now that I was around other people, I'd be okay.

I must have taken longer running away from The Green than I thought, because only a few kids were still eating. The rest of them were probably watching TV in our general rec room, before the afternoon classes started.

I sat down and was given a plate that held potato chips

and a grilled cheese sandwich.

I dug in, and as I did, I saw a new boy sitting by himself at a corner table.

I had never seen him before. It was curious, because the school never just inserted a new student in the middle of a semester. Maybe I was clueless and had never noticed him before.

I was feeling a little more stable by then. My terror from just a few minutes earlier was shrinking to the back of my brain as I focused on this new boy.

Maybe he was meant somehow to distract me from The Green.

An idea came to me as I picked up my plate and sat down next to him. He opened his mouth, maybe to protest or say how gross girls were, like a lot of boys my age did.

But in the end, he settled for smiling politely with a glazed look in his eyes. He seemed to be a really weird boy. Still, I felt like I *should* sit here, that I should try to be his friend. Something about him said he *needed* companionship.

"Hi," I said. "I'm Loralee."

He gave me a very strange, far-away look. Did I offend him by speaking to him? Whenever *I* had a look like that, my father would say, "A penny for your thoughts."

Now I paused and reflected on my father. I missed him so much. It seemed like it had been so long since I'd looked at his face and had his arms around me, making me feel safe.

I sighed and looked again at the quiet boy. I considered saying "A penny for your thoughts" to this boy too, but then I changed my mind. I had just barely met him. Would it be correct to say that to someone you'd just met? He might have thought I was a little too friendly.

"Harrison." He finally introduced himself. He wasn't smiling. And he was still giving me that odd look.

But I smiled back and continued eating. I was so hungry after what had just happened in the halls.

I was halfway through my grilled cheese sandwich before I decided to attempt more conversation. "Why aren't you eating?"

Okay, it wasn't really conversation so much as a nosy question. And on second thought, I did realize how peculiar it was that he didn't have any food with him. Why was he even in the dining hall if he wasn't going to eat?

Benny entered the dining hall. He was adorable with light brown hair. He had been in some terrible accident years ago and now wore an eye patch over one eye, which was strange for someone my age. I'd never asked him about it, but I wondered about it every time I looked at his face.

As Benny walked near our table, Harrison – who was stretching his arms out behind him – accidentally hit Benny's torso. That light jab somehow made Benny fall back and drop to the ground.

Benny must have been daydreaming or totally out of it somehow.

Worried, I went over to Benny to help him up. He didn't seem very willing to get up on his own, so I had to practically pick him up. Then, we just looked at each other for a few seconds, and Benny smiled at me – the same smile he always gave me – and continued on his way.

I turned to ask Harrison if he was okay. I reached an arm out to touch his shoulder in a soothing way, but he just looked at my hand as if spiders were crawling all over it. There was an awkward silence. Not knowing what else to do, I put my arm down and returned to my seat.

Finally, he cleared his throat, his eyes shooting over to me finally. "Just don't touch me," he whispered, so quietly that I wondered if he was talking to himself and not me.

"Uh… okay," I told him, a question clearly in my voice. I was no expert, but that sounded pretty suspicious to me. It was weird for *anyone* to say. What did he mean? Why did he act so strangely?

"So," I began again, taking control and trying to involve him in a nice, normal conversation. "When did you get here at Wittenkey Boarding School?"

Again, he just stared at me instead of immediately answering. Why did he communicate with people this way? Was he one of those people who needed a lot more time and attention before he could fully retain information? If that was the case, how in the world did he get accepted to Wittenkey? It wasn't a public school, you know. Not just anyone could attend.

Finally, his eyes lit up and he seemed to understand my question. "Uh, not too long ago, I guess," he answered. He was avoiding my eyes now. I didn't know why, but it intrigued me even more.

I pursed my lips together. I did that a lot when I was annoyed or frustrated. Harrison's eyes darted back over to me. He saw the look on his face and he actually smiled.

I liked his smile. It made me feel peaceful.

"I know someone who liked to make that face you're making right now," he said. Strange. He was clearly my age, but something about the way he spoke reminded me of an older person, like someone as old as my dad. His tone was jovial at first, and right after that it became really sad. He looked off into the distance as if he saw something I didn't. He was *wistful*. He looked sadder every moment.

I felt like I should have said something. I decided on asking a straightforward question, seeing as how I'd been pretty polite so far. Maybe that gave me informal permission to be a little direct now. "Why do you look so sad?"

He was obviously in outer space, perhaps hopping along the surface of one of Jupiter's moons in his obviously-disturbed brain. "Please."

That was all he said, without turning to face me. Was that a reply? I was confused.

He just sat there, and we were both silent for a while.

"Please what?" I asked, holding the last few bites of my sandwich, which I was now ignoring. This new boy was so distracting and strange.

"Please."

Again, that was all he said. I was starting to get mad, because I hated it when people didn't answer my questions.

My sandwich dropped to the floor as my fingers loosened around it. Drat! I was so hungry still. Maybe I could talk the dorm parent or *someone* into giving me another one.

I scooted my butt a little further away from Harrison so that I could bend down and pick up my floor-wich. It was filthy. My mother would have had a fit if she were here to witness this.

After cleaning my mess I sat there next to him in silence for a while. He was in his own world, so I struggled for something to say.

"Is there something you want to talk about?" I asked him quietly.

Tears overflowed the rims of his eyes but somehow didn't

escape. "I can't talk about it," he said, barely able to choke out the words.

And then he got up and walked away, leaving me there at the table by myself.

I sat there a little surprised because it's pretty rude to leave someone alone at a table. What was it that he couldn't talk about, and why was he saying 'please' so much? I became intrigued with these thoughts so much that eating was now the last thing on my mind. I never did get that replacement sandwich. Too bad, because grilled cheese was my absolute favorite.

The rest of my day at school was pretty boring, and no one else attempted much discussion with me. See, even though I was so very popular, a lot of girls didn't like how smart I was or how rich my family was. They stayed away from me, standing in groups between classes, gossiping and turning their heads to look at me every so often. I didn't care, though. I really preferred to keep to myself.

I headed back to my room with some illustrations I'd made during art class. I got to my room, looked at the insipid paper plate I'd drawn on and threw it out, laughing at it as I did so. It was such a pathetic piece. I wished my art teacher would let us do more elaborate things. I'd be up for the challenge, you see. I was very good at art. But I guess she just wanted everyone in class to be able to keep up, and I could understand that.

I spent the rest of the afternoon reading some classic literature. But once it started to get dark, I began to panic. Today was Wednesday, and The Green would be coming back for me tonight.

I was afraid. I was *so* very afraid of The Green.

As evening approached I had my supper, washed up, and put on my PJs. I also left my dorm light on. We weren't supposed to do that, but at that moment I didn't care about school rules. I actually hoped they'd bust me so that security could come into my room in the middle of the night and rescue me from the horror that inevitably awaited me.

I just needed to protect myself against The Green, and being able to see everything in my room seemed to be a no-brainer. Quietly, slowly, I lifted up the covers of my small bed, peering inside to make sure there wasn't anything sinister lying underneath the blankets waiting for me. All I saw was the blanket and mattress.

It was all clear.

I got in my bed but did not lie down. I sat where my head should have been, and I brought my knees up to my face. I hugged my knees after covering myself with my blankets and leaned my tired head back against the wall behind me.

I was like that for so long that I began to nod off.

But I woke up when the light went out!

My room was pitch-dark now. Except for a small sliver of light coming from underneath the door from the lit hallway. I wanted to get up, to walk over to where the switch was to turn my light back on, but what if it didn't work? What if I had to just stand there in the dark, vulnerable to The Green's attack?

The decision was made. I was not getting up.

I wouldn't have been able to do it anyway. My body was too frozen to attempt such a mission.

A paper rustled somewhere in my room.

I gasped, my body coming to life. I scooted my body back even more, wishing I could melt into the wall. At least then I'd be safe.

I was breathing hard through my mouth. This way I could

listen for any more sounds that might have come up. I was looking toward my front door, which was still shut.

I felt my body beginning to tremble from fear. I was amazed that I hadn't died from fright yet. I was also amazed that I survived the terror I experienced every week from The Green.

My room was as dark and quiet as a tomb. I continued to press myself into the wall behind me. Tears were now streaming quickly down my face, as if the drops were racing each other.

I then realized that some noise might have been good after all. There was one noise in particular that might have helped. Slowly, I put the edges of my blanket under my armpits to hold it around me. I reached up to my forehead to do the sign of the cross.

My prayer was whispered. I was saying this slowly so I could still listen for sounds. "Our Father, who art in Heaven, hallowed be Thy name…"

Movement in the corner of my eye.

My heart started pounding. I turned my head toward the movement. Nothing there.

"Thy kingdom come, Thy will be done…"

A small lump appeared under the blanket, at the foot of my bed.

I was not breathing at all now. I wondered if The Green would kill me quickly. I hoped it would.

The lump grew bigger. It was the size of a cat now.

I was sobbing, but I was trying so very hard to finish my prayer. "On Earth as it…i-i-is in…Heaven."

The lump has grown bigger. Much, much bigger.

It was moving across my tiny bed.

Toward me. But there was nowhere for me to go. I was

cornered.

Something freezing and slippery grabbed my wrist. I heard a voice that sounded more like the growl of a giant lion. It was as if I were watching a movie with the stereo system turned all the way up.

"LORALEE!"

Its voice was deafening. I screamed and squeezed my eyes shut. I tried to finish my prayer but suddenly couldn't remember it.

I didn't see it, but I knew what it looked like. I'd seen it once before with my naked eye, and every night thereafter in my haunted dreams. It sort of looked like Bigfoot but a see-through version, and there was a forest-green color to it.

Its face and body were blank. Literally blank, with no features or skin color or scars or anything, much like the surface of a chalkboard. It had no nose, no eyes, no ears, no hair. It was just a gigantic green shadowy mass.

With just one grotesque detail.

On its face – or face *area*, to be more accurate – was an enormous, clown-like smile. That was the only thing I could see or remember about it. That blasted smile. I didn't know what The Green's teeth looked like because its mouth was closed. It was just an unnaturally wide smile. Remembering that smile, I remembered something. There was more to The Green than this weekly terror. But cowering there on my bed at this moment, praying, crying, and covering my head with my hands, I truly couldn't recall where.

It howled an inhuman laugh into the air. It was much more ferocious than the hideous laugh I'd heard earlier at lunchtime. Bright bursts of pain stabbed at my throat repeatedly, but I fought it. I finally began screaming and pleading, still not looking at the wretchedness in front of me.

And then, after enduring my waking nightmare, finally, thankfully, there was nothing.

I opened my eyes to my dorm room that was softly lit from the rising sun outside my window.

I was lying in a weird position on my bed, across it horizontally with my head almost completely off the bed.

I sat up slowly. I felt a little more relaxed at first after a full night's sleep, but then as I remembered the terror I went through last night, my anxiety returned.

My throat was throbbing with pain. I started to cry out, but that just made the pain increase a hundredfold. Did The Green stab my throat again with those mini-swords it always seemed to have?

Why didn't it just kill me? I couldn't live another week in fear of it.

I began to sob, the unbearable pain wrapping around my throat like a collar. I cried again, this time from shock, although why it surprised me at all was anyone's guess.

I should have been used to this by now.

Sluggishly, I stood up and walked towards my door. I had a small mirror hanging next to it, so I approached it and took a look at myself.

There were bruises all around my throat.

I cried silently as I got dressed, glad I had the option of wearing a turtleneck. My tears stained the shirt as I pulled my head through.

I tried talking to Tara about The Green at breakfast in the

dining hall later. But she was no help. None at all! She told me it didn't exist.

"Well, you are wrong!" I shouted to her. "It exists. I have the bruises to prove it."

She kept shaking her head, her long blond dreadlocks swaying back and forth around her head. It distracted me for a moment. I wanted to ask her how she could possibly get away with that hairstyle knowing how strict the school's dress code was.

But I didn't. Instead, I asked her what she thought, and she said something that I didn't quite understand.

"Well, if this Green of yours does exist, you must try to remember." She looked at me carefully, her blue eyes so crystal clear.

"What in the world are you talking about, Tara? Remember what?"

"Why it's mad at you." Her voice dropped to a whisper now. "What you did."

I looked down at her plate and realize she wasn't eating very much. Why doesn't anybody around here ever eat? And then I realized what she'd just said.

"What I did?" She nodded and I sat there, frustrated and pondering. "Burning the animals a long time ago, you mean?"

"No!" Tara exclaimed loudly. "You really don't remember? What is wrong with you, Loralee?"

I sat back and shook my head to myself. "I wish I knew. How I wish I knew!"

Tara went back to nibbling at her breakfast daintily, and I knew our conversation was over. I was done with my breakfast, so I got up, planning to watch TV in the rec room until it was time for class.

But I saw Harrison sitting at a table alone, not eating, as usual. Watching me. His face expressionless.

Yet…something about him made me want to sit next to him again. He didn't seem surprised.

"Hi," I told him.

"She's right, you know," he said.

"Who?"

He motioned his head to where Tara was sitting. "Your… uh…friend. If that's what she is," he replied.

I was shocked by his words. "You don't think Tara's my friend?"

He merely sighed. "That's not important, Loralee. I'm just saying she's right. You should remember why The Green is mad at you. You should remember what you did."

"Why are you speaking to me as if you've known me my whole life? How do you know about The Green? You just got here!"

He finally gave me a smile, and it really relaxed me. Automatically, I smiled back at him. "It isn't that hard to overhear you," he said.

"Oh." I looked around and realized the dining hall was nearly empty now.

"Look, Loralee." He looked at me hard in my eyes. "You need to remember everything, because I can help you get out of here. And then they can't hurt you anymore. But I need you aware and back to being yourself."

They?

I got mad. "You are clearly insane," I told him, standing up and smoothing my school uniform. "Harrison, I don't know you, okay? You don't know me, and you don't know what I've been through in my thirteen years."

"Thirteen?" Harrison's confused again, and he was looking at me like I was insane.

Like *I* was insane! Ha! Ironic.

He stood up slowly, but it was so deliberate that somehow, it scared me. "Loralee, you are twenty-eight years old. I'm sorry if that's a harsh reality check for you, but you need it."

Now I was really pissed off. I started yelling. I did not know why. This boy was obviously spouting lies. I threw the rest of my breakfast at the wall. I didn't know if anyone was watching and I didn't care. "What are you going to tell me next, that this isn't a school?" I gestured my arms around to indicate the dining hall where we sat.

He seemed to consider. "Well, it technically is a school, but..."

I didn't want to hear anymore. I got up and ran out the door and into the hall. After a minute, I stopped because I saw Benny standing there in the middle of the hallway.

Benny just smiled at me the way he always did. "What are you doing out here by yourself?" he asked me. "Come on, I'll walk you back to the dining hall."

"But I don't need to go back to–" I started to say, but it was too late. He was already walking away, and I followed him.

After a couple minutes of silence, he asked, "You know, right?"

This was why I loved Benny so much. He always knew what was on my mind. He would always be special to me. I couldn't imagine living my life without him. I looked at Benny warily, and I sighed because I was about to say something out loud. Something I always pretended I didn't know.

He opened the door for me and I stepped through to the dining hall. We stood there, talking. I knew what Benny was talking about. I knew *exactly* what he was talking about.

I had been in denial.

"You're referring to the fact that Wittenkey is actually a school for the emotionally disturbed and not the intellectually gifted? That *I* am emotionally disturbed? That we're in Montana, and not New York?" I paused, then slumped my shoulders and added, "Yeah, Benny, I know."

I sighed and paced in a circle around Benny. This was one of those few times that I wished I smoked cigarettes, because that sounded like a fun thing to do while walking laps around your best friend. "I know I'm different. I know what I fantasize about doing, and it sure ain't getting naked with boys," I continued.

Benny just smiled at me the way he always does. "No, Loralee. I'm referring to the fact that I'm just a teddy bear."

I looked at him as I gasped and blinked my eyes.

My world shifted, almost as if I had entered an alternate universe, but sadly, it was reality. My reality. My world as it truly existed.

Also known as Hell on Earth.

My vision got blurry as the world around me spun in circles. When it cleared, I saw that I was in what probably once was a large rec room. I saw the peeling, browning wallpaper.

The second thing that I noticed was the smell. It smelled like a combination of rotting wood, moldy walls, and something else that I really could not and would not want to place. I was still for a moment as I looked at the room as it truly was. There was a piano with half the keys missing that sat off to the side next to the only window. The rest of the room was empty. The floor was caked with dust, and many tiles were missing.

And then I felt Benny standing behind me.

I turned around slowly, my eyes landing on the adorable teddy bear with the light brown fur that I'd played with for years, right down to his missing button-eye. I wept silently as I picked him up and hugged him tight.

As I wept, I saw a mop leaning vertically in the corner, its coarse lengths of yarn hanging limply. The yarn vaguely resembled dreadlocks.

Tara.

That was Tara.

And Harrison?

I turned around the other way, still clutching Benny to my chest. I realized that I was a lot taller than I'd thought. I had a woman's body.

But I forgot all about this once I saw Harrison.

I screamed and dropped Benny, scrambling backwards toward the broken-down piano.

I could see through Harrison. He was a ghost.

I began bawling. "Who are you? Who are you?"

"You need to remember, Loralee," he said again. He approached me slowly, as if I were a wild animal. "I'm not going to hurt you," he whispered.

"You're my responsibility," he whispered, more to himself than to me. "Neither one of us should have ended up this way." He put a hand to his forehead and closed his eyes for a moment. He opened them and continued, "I will be here until the day you die, and then I will lead you into paradise. That's the least I can do for you, after all you've done for me."

I was hunched over on the floor. I did not know what to say or do.

Harrison continued. "I know that somewhere inside, you're a gentle spirit. I will always believe in you, Loralee."

He knelt in front of me, and suddenly he looked different. He didn't look expressionless. He looked alive, fleshy, and real.

He also looked terrified. "Please."

There was that please again. But there was something different about how he said it this time. Like he was showing me something important.

So I watched.

He talked again. "Please. I can't go another day."

I gasped loudly. Those were the magic words.

I finally did remember everything then, but it didn't matter because somehow, Harrison was showing me everything else that I'd forgotten. We were reenacting what happened the last time we were together, alive.

And I was really glad, because I didn't ever want to forget my favorite cousin.

"Please kill me," he said. He was hunched over, shivering, although it was not cold here. He met my eyes, and I saw that his own eyes were terror-stricken. To make matters worse, his pants were loose. As if he had gone for a whole day without wearing pants and had just slipped them on in a hurry before coming over to my parents' house.

What was he doing with his pants barely on? And why did he want to die?

Suddenly, my lunch lurched in my throat. I understood exactly what happened, because I knew how crazy my aunt and uncle were. I knew what my they did to my cousin. What they did every night to him. Thinking about it, I realized I'd always known.

I suddenly felt like *I* was the one who wanted to die. "I can't kill you," I whimpered, scared. "I would go to Hell." My voice lowered down to a whisper. I shook my head repeatedly. "I can't."

He tilted his head up a little, and the sun placed a soft spotlight on his eyes and on the tears that cascaded down his cheeks. It hurt me. It almost literally broke my heart. I did not know how I could ever trust another human being after knowing what unspeakable acts Harrison's parents had been doing to him. I wished I could take away his pain.

"You might," he agreed. His voice was a slow and sad whisper. "But I need you, Loralee. Please. I can't go another day..." he broke out into sobs, and it was not long before I joined him, the sound of our collective weeping formulating an eerie yet profound melody.

He reached into his backpack and pulled out a knife. I moaned and screamed at the same time, falling to my side and still sobbing. "How can you ask me this? I don't want to torture you."

"I know what 'torture' means," he responded, "And you, Loralee, can't give it to me. I am tortured every night. And nothing could be worse. Your stabs would be a blessing. So please," he looked up at me again.

Something came over me. I was not thinking, but I was acting. Suddenly I wanted to grip that knife in my hands, and I wanted to smell the beautiful metallic odor of fresh blood.

I grabbed the knife from him and I plunged it into his chest, not stopping to ask if he was still alive, because if he was, he was in a kind of pain that I couldn't ever imagine. So I kept stabbing over and over, my throat creating a strange, animalistic sound.

Harrison cried, but only a little bit. I was still in a frenzy, stabbing him until I realized that he wasn't moving anymore. It was a long time before I let up. I smelled blood, and it made me smile a little.

It felt like I was covered with a layer of sweat, but when I felt my arms stick to my sides, I looked down and saw that I was covered in a layer of blood. Harrison's blood. There was so much that it looked like my own throat was cut or like I butchered pigs for a living, although the fun I had with the small animals of the neighborhood wasn't too far off. I'd been soaked in another living thing's blood before, just not a person.

And then I looked back at my cousin. He was still. He was not moving or breathing.

But he *was* wearing a soft smile.

Harrison was gone. He was at peace, but I…was not. Actually, I had a feeling my own turmoil had just begun.

That night, back in my own reality in the present day, I was struggling against The Green again. I did not know why; it was not Wednesday. It was Thursday.

There were *two* Greens this time. Things were starting to make more sense now that I remembered the truth about the psychosis that ran in my family.

"We're going to do this every night now. Forget the once-a-week shit," one Green was saying to the other. It was speaking as if I were a piece of furniture in the room. "I can't believe she's remembering her real age and what happened to Harrison. The more she remembers, the better chance she has of escaping. Take her journal too. I don't want her to keep track of anything."

No! I needed that journal to keep track of my memories, to piece together my fragmented mind. Every DAY I would have to remember Harrison?

"I'll take her journal in the morning," the other Green responded. "Let the bitch write her final words, so we can read them for ourselves, over and over."

"And up her acid intake and her other meds. She should have been tripping big time by now," the first Green growled.

Who were they? I was just about to figure it out, but they closed the lights, and then I could see nothing.

"Please," I said. "I don't want to forget Harrison. He's all I have left."

There was a pause, and then the first Green answered me in the dark. "Harrison has been dead for a long time, my dear."

Now I screamed as loud as I can. "Don't take away my memories! It took so long to remember! Stop!"

Pills were being shoved into my mouth and forced down my throat. God, it hurt. My throat would probably have bruises once again.

I wanted to tell those Greens that they couldn't do this against my will. That I was getting stronger for every moment I was off these damn drugs. I wanted to remember not to eat the food they gave me. Most importantly, I wanted to tell them that I would continue to talk to my cousin's ghost until the day I died and the two of us could go to Heaven.

Just as Harrison promised.

But suddenly my tongue didn't work too well. I could not formulate any words.

My brain was slowing down, too. My eyelids were heavy. It was hard to write these very words. They had left and I was writing in the dark. But I must persevere. I must record everything so I could plan a way out of this physical and mental prison.

Oh, god. I just couldn't stay awake. I'd have to continue my plan in the morning. Good night, diary.

I woke up with this journal right next to me, so the first thing I did was write in it.

I felt groggy but happy.

I wanted to read what I'd written in this journal so far, because I couldn't seem to remember very much.

Some friends just stepped into my dorm room with me. They'd knocked a minute ago, and I let them in. They were telling me that they would enter my journal in a writing contest for English class. I was so excited! I guess I would have to wait to read my journal. They are standing here waiting for me to finish. I'll just read it later when they return it to me.

Until, then, diary, I'll tell you a bit about myself.

I go to one of the best boarding schools in the country. I am 13 years old. My name is Loralee.

~*~

Dr. Greene walked inside the huge empty building, his steps sounding more like hollow clumps. It had once been a great boarding school, but for the last fifteen years it's been devoid of children, laughter, and life.

He held the diary with his right hand, the book splayed open. He snapped the book shut, the sound becoming something of a sonic boom that echoed through the empty place.

It was a good idea of his wife's, to dress up in jeans and wear backpacks, thus disguising themselves as teenagers. They'd lied to Loralee to get her diary away from her. She had been remembering, they could tell, but they had no idea how.

And now she would never remember. They'd have to increase her doses.

Dr. Greene walked over to the second floor to Loralee's room where he'd installed a two-way mirror. Loralee was almost thirty years old now. His wife, Mrs. Greene, approached the mirror as well. After a brief nod to her husband, they both turned to examine Loralee. There she was, talking excitedly to her teddy bear and that stupid dirty mop, and to some more invisible friends. Apparently, she's been tripping so hard that she'd thought she was seeing Harrison's ghost.

The idea was laughable. Ghosts don't exist.

The couple watched as she spoke in different pitches on behalf of the inanimate objects.

That rancid bitch was responsible for Harrison's death. Their beloved son was gone. They had discussed it, 15 years ago, when their niece first murdered Harrison, claiming that she'd done it to save him from *them.* From his own parents! What did *she* know about their love for Harrison? She had no right to interfere. Harrison was *their* property, and she'd taken him away.

While they'd mourned, they had quickly agreed that Loralee should suffer a fate worse than death.

Torture. For as long as they both shall live.

Yes. Harrison was gone forever, but Loralee had taken his place. They would do everything to her that they'd done to him and more. Loralee was already a disturbed child, exhibiting early signs of psychosis, but with the LSD they slipped in her food and the huge pills that they forced down her throat once a week – daily now – she would always be their prisoner.

Husband and wife looked at each other now. They exchanged triumphant grins. They didn't need to speak to each other to know that they were both thinking of how they'd take turns forcing her to take her damn pills, sometimes punching her in the throat to accomplish just that. They found it amusing that Loralee viewed them as one, one monster-ghost, to be exact. They loved that her mind was stuck at age thirteen. It served her right.

"We have many more games to play with our dear Loralee," Mrs. Greene commented.

"Oh, yes," Dr. Greene agreed. "It will never end for her. I can promise you that."

He smiled a huge unnatural grin as they walked down the rotting halls together.

GHOST WRITER

Michael Hillcrest

"A writing retreat. This is such a great idea." Carly looked through the windshield of Matt's fixed-up Mustang. Montchartes Manor was just visible through the palmetto trees lining the boulevard. "I'm so glad you suggested this."

She reached over and grabbed Matt's hand. He squeezed it back.

"We deserve it," he said without taking his eyes from the road. "We're both really close. We're about to break through, get an agent, land with a big house. This is just what we need. A weekend of writing, sharing ideas, and..."

He let his thought trail off.

Carly squeezed his hand. "I'm looking forward to the 'and...' too," she giggled. "Three days should be enough for plenty of that and some writing too."

The car pulled into the drive for the manor. It was really more 'big, old house' than 'manor', but the name had stuck somehow. Now it was a B&B just far enough out of town to offer the promise of some solitude.

"How did you find this place?" asked Carly, craning forward to get a better view of their impending lodgings.

"Internet," Matt replied. "I did a search for 'writing re-treats charleston' and this popped up at the top of the list."

He parked the car in the gravel lot on the side of the tur-reted and gabled home and they both stepped out into the warm afternoon.

"I wonder why this was first," considered Carly.

"Don't you know?" Matt asked as he retrieved their bags and laptops from the trunk. "Helen Montchartes was a writer—or a wanna-be writer anyway. She shut herself up in here, working on her version on the great American novel. She actually died sit-ting at her typewriter."

"Helen Montchartes?" Carly tried the name. "Never heard of her."

Matt laughed. "No surprise there. I guess she was a pretty crappy writer."

He put his arm around his girlfriend. "Come on. Let's see if we can channel some of that bad writing energy."

~*~

The floor of the foyer-turned-lobby creaked almost as much as the boards on the front porch. Dusty beams of light filtered onto the reception desk, where a heavy-set woman sat in front of a punchboard holding a half dozen room keys. She was watching a small television but stood up and smiled warmly when Matt and Carly entered.

"Hello. Welcome to Montchartes Manor."

"Thanks," replied Matt as he stepped up to the counter. Carly started examining the frames hanging on the walls.

"We have a reservation," Matt started. "The name is—"

"I have your reservation right here, young man," the woman interrupted. "You're our only guests this weekend. Unless something unexpected happens."

Matt smiled. He had an idea. "This was Helen Montchartes home, wasn't it?"

"Exactly. Author Helen Montchartes." Her emphasis on the title undermined its force.

"Is her room available?" Matt asked in a lowered voice. "You know, since no one else will be here anyway."

The woman's smile didn't fade exactly, but it changed. "Her room *is* available," she answered slowly, "but we rarely rent it out. Ms. Montchartes, well, she passed away in her room, bent over her typewriter, still writing until the very end."

Matt smiled even more broadly. "I knew that actually. I'm a writer too." Then, almost an afterthought, he added, "And so is my girlfriend."

"Hey, Matt," Carly called over her shoulder. "Come see this."

Matt offered the reception lady an 'excuse me' smile and stepped over to Carly.

Carly pointed at several framed documents hanging on the wall. "These are her rejection letters. From all the publishing houses she submitted to."

There were dozens of them. Each covered in marks and comments, ostensibly from Helen's own hand. The typical, boiler-plate compliments—'while I like the premise...' and 'you have a strong voice but...' and 'although your prose is crisp and enga-ging...'—were underlined, or doubled underlined, or even circled and starred. But the critiques—'the story failed to grab me...' and 'the characterization was weak...' and 'this just isn't for me...'—we're scratched over, sometimes scribbled out, and usually accompanied by a diatribe in the margin where Helen felt compelled to argue the point.

"Wow," said Matt. "Guess she didn't like getting rejected."

Carly just nodded. "She should be glad she got any response at all. We usually just close them out after a couple months."

Matt laughed. "Yeah, well, some people take all the rejection pretty personally."

He gave Carly a quick hug and stepped back to the reception desk. The woman was waiting for him, a stack of towels extended with a room key on top.

"Enjoy Ms. Montchartes' room," she said. "I think she'd want you to have it."

~*~

The room was really the home's attic. It encompassed the entire floor, with gables for reading nooks, and a turret for a library.

"Oh, Matt!" Carly swept into the room. "It's gorgeous."

Matt smiled and nodded approvingly as he set their bags on the brass bed with a squeak. "Yeah, just the place to scare up some writing spirits."

As Carly sampled the view from each window, Matt stepped over to the old roll-top desk against the far wall. The top was down, but Matt didn't hesitate at all to lift it, exposing the antique typewriter beneath. It was classic black with chrome accents and circular letter keys jutting up over the machine's exposed intestines. There was even a stack of brittle typing paper lined up perfectly next to it. Matt lifted a sheet and tucked it into the contraption, turning the carriage roller to bring the page up under the ribbon.

"Hey, look at me," he called out, taking a seat in the creaky desk chair. "I'm Earnest Hemingway."

He grinned over his shoulder at Carly who was unpacking her own writing tool: a refurbished laptop she'd found online. She plugged it into the wall and folded up the screen. "Stop fooling around, Matt. You're likely to break something."

Matt's smile broadened as he ignored his girlfriend's admonition and set his fingers on the keys.

"It," he quoted as he typed, "was a dark and stormy— Oh, damn."

"It was a dark and stormy damn?" Carly laughed. "Are you sure that's how it goes?"

Matt frowned. "No, the 'm' key stuck," he explained. "It was a dark and storm. That's all I could type." He curled a finger under the 'm' key's lever and pulled it from the carriage. "How could anybody write a novel on one of these things? I would get so frustrated."

Carly tapped her laptop as the start chime spilled from its speaker. "The keys on this thing stick sometimes too. Except when that happens the same letter comes out like a billion times. I would have written, 'It was a dark and stormmmmmmmmm.'"

Matt laughed and stood up with another creak from the chair. "Well, yeah, that's pretty irritating too. So, do you think this is *the* typewriter?"

Carly stepped over to look. "What do you mean, '*the* typewriter'?"

"The one she died over," Matt explained with a bit too much gleam in his eye.

Carly's eyes held no gleam. "I sure as hell hope not. That's too creepy. You better not have brought me to the room where some old lady croaked over her typewriter. No way you're getting any if this room is haunted or something."

Matt immediately regretted his interest in Helen Montchartes' death. Or rather, he regretted giving voice to it. "Oh, no, don't worry. I asked the lady at the front desk. She said that room is never rented out. I just wondered if they maybe moved the typewriter in here. You know, for atmosphere."

Carly's expression let him know she didn't really believe him. Luckily, he was saved from further interrogation by the sound of a 'new email' alert from Carly's computer. She turned slowly, holding her doubtful gaze on her boyfriend as long as she could, then stepped over to her laptop.

Matt quickly lowered the roll-top—just as Carly screamed. "Ahhh!"

"What is it?" Matt rushed over to her.

"I got a full request!" Carly squealed. "A full manuscript request! From Eva Margolis! Eva fucking Margolis!"

Matt new the name of course. Eva Margolis was one of the biggest literary agents in New York. She had rejected a half dozen of his manuscripts. Or he supposed she had; she'd never shown the courtesy to send even a form rejection.

"Wow," said Matt, swallowing the hateful bile forcing itself up his throat. "That's, that's great."

Carly was still staring at the screen, doing little jumps in place with both hands over her mouth. "I got a full request from Eva fucking Margolis!"

Matt forced a smile and patted Carly on the back, but more to get her to stop the annoying mini-jumps than to congratulate her. "That's great," he repeated. "You can send it to her first thing Monday."

"Monday?!" Carly finally pulled her gaze from the computer but only to offer the most incredulous of looks. "Are you crazy? I'm sending it right now."

Matt frowned. "I thought we were going to go for a walk?"

"You can go for a walk," she snapped. "I'm sending the full. Now."

When Matt didn't reply, Carly widened her eyes and held two open palms toward her laptop. "Eva. Fucking. Margolis."

Matt finally forced a smile. "Right, right. Got it." He patted her arm. "You go ahead and send it. I'll meet you out on the porch."

Carly spun back to her laptop and started typing. Matt stepped to the door. The bile was no longer trying to come up his throat. It was burning a nice little hole in his gut.

~*~

Matt was glad he'd waited for Carly on the porch, as a walk in the sunshine turned out to be just the thing for both of them. The warmth of the day chased away the caustic mood in Matt, and the beauty of the day finally succeeded in getting Carly to talk about something other than Eva fucking Margolis. By the time they returned to the B&B for dinner, Matt had almost forgotten about Carly's full request. Almost.

"You know you can't get your hopes up," he practically slapped her with the words. "I mean, the odds against an offer are astronomical."

Carly winced at the affront. "Thanks for the vote of confidence, Matt."

"I'm sorry, honey," Matt said when he saw the look in Carly's eye. "That's not what I meant. It's just that I don't want to see you get your hopes up, only to get hurt."

The sparkle returned to Carly's eyes. "You know me better than that, Matt. I'm tough. Hell, I can be downright ruthless when I want. Eva fucking Margolis will make me an offer of representation, or else she's an idiot."

Matt's cautious smile blossomed into a full and relaxed one. "There you go. And you're right. If she doesn't see how good you're writing is, then fuck her. She doesn't know talent when she sees it. You're a damn good writer. She'd be lucky to rep you."

Carly's smile changed too, but less innocently. She reached out and took Matt's hand. "Thank you, Matt. Now why don't we head upstairs?"

Matt's other hand was in the air instantaneously. "Check, please!"

The front-desk lady waddled over to them. She was the cook and waitress too. In fact, she appeared to be the only employee at all.

"There's no check, young man. We'll just add it to your bill."

"Oh, great. Thanks." He started to get up, then realized he had a question. "Um, if we need anything later tonight—new towels, new ... sheets"—Carly giggled—"Do we just call down to you?"

The woman offered a pencil-thin smile. "I'm afraid not, sir. I don't spend the night here. You'll be on your own until daybreak. Morning, that is. I'll check on you when I come in."

Matt furrowed his brow at the idea of being completely alone in the house all night. But before he decided whether to say anything, the woman finished with, "Don't you worry, though. There are plenty of extra linens in the hall closet."

Then she looked out the window, past the clock on the

wall, and announced, "In fact, it's starting to get dark out. I'll be leaving soon. You kids have a good night."

Carly squeezed Matt's hand. "Oh, we will. Thank you, ma'am. See you tomorrow."

Matt was still unsure, but Carly eased his troubled mind. "All alone, all night," she purred. "We can be as loud as we want."

Matt's heart raced and he forgot whatever it was he had been concerned about. He squeezed Carly's hand back, then stood up. "Come on," he said. "Let's see how squeaky that old bed really is."

~*~

Upstairs, after some passionate kissing through the doorway, Matt slipped into attached attic bathroom. He emptied his bladder and appraised himself in the mirror. He wasn't the handsomest man in the world, he knew, but he was okay-looking. Besides, Carly liked how he looked, and that was all that mattered. He smiled at himself, then opened the door, ready to throw down with his girlfriend.

Instead, he threw his hands down on his thighs. "Carly! What are you doing?"

What she was doing was obvious. She was checking her email on her laptop.

"Sorry, Matt. I just had to check." She shrugged. "But no word back yet from Eva fucking Margolis."

Matt frowned. "Of course not. It's only been a few hours since you sent her a seventy-five-thousand word manuscript. It's not like she's going to drop everything to read it."

Carly shrugged and looked down again at the computer screen. "Yeah, I guess you're right. It's just hard to wait."

Matt stepped in behind her, wrapping his arms around her waist. "Oh, I know. I know." He started kissing the back of her neck. "Now let's stop talking about Eva fucking Margolis, and start talking about Carly fucking Matt."

Carly arched her hips back against her boyfriend. "Mmm, yes, sir."

And their getaway began in earnest.

~*~

The moonlight shone through the drapes and onto Matt's stomach. A sheet covered him below his waist and draped up over Carly's naked hips. She had rolled over after their final lovemaking and fallen asleep as he lay flat on his back, heart still racing, and did the same. But a wind through the window stirred him and he became vaguely aware of his surroundings.

He wasn't sure how long he'd been asleep but he was pleasantly surprised to find Carly had awakened too and was climbing back on top of him. He didn't open his eyes as he felt her body slid onto his. He reached up to touch her face, but she moved his hands to her waist and buried her face into his neck.

It was different. Slower, smoother somehow. There was a refreshing coolness to her skin. And she was silent. Carly was never silent. Matt tried to open his eyes and look at her, but the moonlight was gone and the room was dark. Besides, her hair was covering his face and he didn't want to break the spell by speaking. He matched her rhythm and their bodies melded in silent perfection.

Then Matt heard a beautiful stranger's voice whisper into his ear, "She stole your story." The words jarred him from the dream. When he threw open his eyes, there was no one there. Carly was still rolled over, fast asleep.

He looked all around. The moonlight was back across his sheet-covered stomach. His heart was racing again. He could smell another woman's perfume in the air. And he couldn't shake the echo of what she'd said.

'She stole your story.'

~*~

Matt had had trouble falling back to sleep, so he woke up later than he'd wanted. When he finally did drift back to consciousness, he reached out for Carly.

But she wasn't there.

Propping himself up on one elbow, he saw her sitting at her table, laptop open, hands over her mouth, and her feet bouncing up and down a mile a minute.

"What is it, hon?" he croaked in that first-words-of-the-day voice.

"An R and R!" Carly squealed through her hands without even looking at him. "A request to revise and resubmit from Eva fucking Margolis."

She finally turned to look at Matt. "She said she loved it. Just needs a few tweaks. Said if I could fix a few areas where the voice wasn't quite right..." but she trailed off and looked back at her screen. "An R and R from Eva fucking Margolis!"

Matt forced a smile. He hadn't ever expected Carly to hit it big. At least, he expected he'd do it first, then maybe help her. His gut burned a bit, but he ignored it and swung his feet out of bed. He had expected they would mess around again in the morning, so he hadn't put any underwear back on. But now, seeing her back in Eva fucking Margolis mode, he pulled out a pair of boxers from his bag and slipped them on as he stumbled over to Carly.

"So which story is it?" he asked. "'Summer In Tuscany'?"

"Hm?" Carly jerked a glance at Matt approaching, then her hands flashed across the keyboard, closing the manuscript and leaving the desktop picture up. It was a generic image of some kittens. Matt was pretty sure it used to be a picture of them on their last camping trip. "Uh, no," she flustered. "It's a new one, called, um, 'Pyromancer.'"

Matt was taken aback. "'Pyromancer'? Huh. Sounds like something I'd write."

"Yeah, it kind of does," Carly replied, bouncing up from her chair and wrapping her arms around Matt's neck. "But I could never write like you."

She kissed him. "Come on," she said. "Let's go eat breakfast."

Matt kissed her cheek and hugged her back—only partially so he could crane his neck for a fruitless glimpse of her laptop.

~*~

The morning seemed to drag on forever for Matt. They had agreed—before Eva fucking Margolis and her R and R—to spend that day half-plotting and half-writing. The plan had been to talk through each other's latest projects in the morning, over breakfast and long walks and an early lunch; then spend the afternoon on the mansion's front porch, feet up, laptops open, and ideas flying through fingertips into the manuscript.

But no.

Carly couldn't stop talking about Eva fucking Margolis. She kind of tried not to, but not really. There was the occasional reference to their planned work, but it always circled back to her maybe agent.

"Do you think she'll want to see this one too, even before

it's done?"

"I've heard they don't even want you to write another one while they're contacting publishers, in case they want a sequel or something. Do you think that's true?"

"How long do you think it'd take until I'm on her website under 'My Authors'?"

The worst part wasn't even the questions. It was that she didn't really wait for, or listen to, his answers. By the time they made it to the porch, Matt was on his last nerve.

"Oh!" Carly looked up from her laptop. "I'll need to change my Twitter bio to say 'repped by @EvaMAgent.'"

"Or you could wait to see if she even offers you represent-ation," Matt snarled as he opened his laptop to renew his fight with his current work-in-progress, "and in the meantime, do what I thought we agreed to do this weekend, which was spend time together writing, not me listening to you talk about your not-agent."

He knew he shouldn't have said it. Not the thoughts them-selves; he knew he was right. Just saying them. Now they were going to fight. Sometimes it's better to just shut up, he knew.

Carly stared at him for several seconds. Then she slammed her laptop shut again.

"You know what, Matt?" She stood up. "Sometimes you can be a real asshole."

She stormed off the porch and into the house.

Matt thought about going after her, but he didn't really want to. He sighed and looked down at his own laptop. *Maybe if I made the bad guy a woman,* he thought.

~*~

Matt stayed on the porch all afternoon. He didn't get much

written, but he wasn't ready to face Carly yet either. Eventually though, dinner time arrived. He folded up his laptop and went into the dining room.

Carly was already there, eating. When she saw Matt, she quickly dabbed her mouth, then stood up and left her half eaten dinner at the table.

"Carly..." Matt tried, but she stormed past him without so much as a glance.

Matt shrugged. He had hoped she wouldn't still be angry. She just needed more time, he figured. She had probably moved from being mad at him for what he said to being mad at him for being right about what he said. He supposed by the time he finished dinner, she would be calmed down enough to talk. And then make up.

Just in time for bed. He smiled. The fights, few as they were, always sucked, but the make-up sex was always amazing.

He sat down at Carly's abandoned table and wondered whether they served oysters.

~*~

"Knock, knock." Matt carefully entered the bedroom.

Carly was sitting at her laptop. She didn't acknowledge him. But she didn't storm away either. So that was something.

Matt knew he'd have to swallow his pride to get the ball rolling. "Um, sorry about what I said earlier."

No response from Carly. She kept typing furiously on her computer. Her keystrokes may even have gotten a bit louder.

"I should have been more understanding," Matt pressed on. "I know this is a big deal. Our writing can wait."

That got a reaction, but not the one Matt anticipated.

"That's why you think I'm mad?" Carly crossed her arms.

"You don't even get it, do you?"

He thought he did, but he knew not to say as much. Ball. Rolling. Make up. Sex. He just shrugged, figuring she'd elaborate. She did.

"You got mad at me for making one silly comment about following her on Twitter. You took my high from finally getting noticed by someone who's big time, and crashed it to the ground. I was feeling pretty good about myself until you reminded me how much of a nothing and a failure I am."

She was starting to tear up, but fought it back.

"I know," said Matt. "And I'm sorry. I shouldn't have said those things. I'm excited for you. I really am."

"That's not it, you asshole!" Carly screamed. "You accused me of not working on our project when that's all I did. I got a fucking R and R from Eva Margolis, but instead of spending every minute on that golden opportunity, I chose to spend the morning with you. Instead of locking myself away like I should have done and getting these revisions done as fast as possible, I walked around with *you,* listening to all the problems *you're* having with *your* manuscript! And then, when I make one little comment about the most exciting thing that's ever happened to me writing-wise, you cut me down and say I don't care about you. Well, fuck you, Matthew Anderson."

Matt just stood there, stunned. He hadn't thought of it that way.

"Oh, just get out of here, Matt!" Carly sniffled. "I need to finish these revisions. Just go away."

She went back to her typing, wiping her nose on the back of her hand. Matt stood there for a moment, processing. Then he grabbed a blanket off the bed and headed downstairs to the couch in the lobby.

~*~

Matt dabbled a bit on his laptop, but he couldn't focus. It was getting dark and he was getting tired, mainly from the fight with Carly. The weekend was turning out exactly opposite of what he had planned. They were supposed to write together, not sleep apart. They were supposed to fuck, not fight.

And he was always supposed to land an agent first.

Matt set his laptop aside and stretched out on the couch, the too-thin blanket not quite large enough to cover his entire length.

Eva fucking Margolis wasn't really the problem, she just made it all crystal clear. Despite all his effort, Matt had never gotten more than a request for a partial manuscript from an agent. But Carly got a full request. And then an R and R. All for a manuscript she'd never even told him she was writing.

He curled onto his side and pulled his legs up so the bottom of the blanket actually covered his feet.

The worst part was that he knew Eva fucking Margolis was going to sign Carly, and instead of being Carly's writer boyfriend who Eva could help and maybe even sign, he was going to be Carly's asshole ex-boyfriend that Eva would make sure got blacklisted from every publishing house and literary agency in New York.

Fuck, Matt thought exhaustedly. Then he fell asleep.

~*~

The moonlight disappeared again, but Matt could tell it was the same woman. He could smell that same perfume. It was unique. Classic. Timeless. Like a jazz album or an old movie.

It took a moment for him to realize what was happening.

She was there again. Kissing him. But not on the lips. Her attentions were directed lower, and he had already risen to them. Reaching out, he felt her cool skin and her silky hair. It wasn't Carly, he knew that this time. But he didn't care either. There was something new—a connection, unspoken, but stronger than he'd ever felt with Carly.

He weaved his fingers through her hair and pulled her mouth to his. She kissed him deeply, sending a chill through his entire body. He leaned back on the couch and she lay on top of him again. Whoever she was, she seemed to know what he needed, what he wanted, exactly what he was feeling inside. She anticipated his every move and met it in advance.

He kept his eyes closed, lest she disappear again, but as the rhythm became more intense, and he could sense that he wouldn't last much longer, he opened his eyes to look into eyes filled with a longing that mirrored his own. He knew she understood him more than anyone ever had. He buried his face into her neck and released. She held his head and hugged him until he stopped moving.

When he fell back again, she traced her fingertips over his eyes, bidding them open. She raised her finger and traced a circle in the air. As she did so, the circle ignited into a ring of fire floating between their faces.

"Yours," she said.

Matt understood. "Mine," he agreed.

Then she was gone, the burning circle evaporating into a plume of smoke, and the best love-making session of his life reduced to the glistening on his stomach in the suddenly returned moonlight.

~*~

Matt pushed open the bedroom door as quietly as its aged hinges would allow.

A careful scan of the darkened room confirmed Carly asleep in the bed, and her laptop in sleep mode on the table. Probably waiting for a middle of the night offer or representation from Eva fucking Margolis, Matt supposed ruefully. He crept across the creaky floorboards and slid his hand across the touch pad.

The screen lit up. Matt waited a moment to confirm the extra light hadn't disturbed Carly, then he opened her email and looked for the email exchange with Margolis.

It was right at the top. He scrolled right to the bottom. He didn't give a shit about what Margolis had written. He wanted to see how Carly had described 'Pyromancer' in her original message.

Dear Ms. Margolis:

In a land without sun, she who controls fire controls the world. Elissa Torlofsdotter is the last Pyromancer, a long line of magic-wielding elves from the north country. She is determined to bring back the light and, with it, freedom to the people of Middle Terra. But powerful forces hide in the sunless darkness, more than willing to destroy Elissa and all she loves.

'Pyromancer' is a 100,000-word tour de force that marries high-fantasy with the best of dark dystopian. Below is a full synopsis. May I send you the manuscript?

Sincerely,

Carly Henning

Matt stared at the screen, his stomach filled with not half as much bile as his heart. He didn't need to read the synopsis. He knew the story. He'd written it. 'Ring of Fire' by Matthew Anderson. Carly had told him it was no good, that he'd never get an agent, and to not even bother querying it. He'd believed her.

Damn it, he'd believed her.

~*~

Matt was waiting for Carly at the bedroom door when she opened it. He had flowers. And the biggest 'I'm sorry, I'm a jerk, please forgive me' smile he could muster.

Carly frowned. "I'm still mad, Matt." But there was something in her tone that let him know the edge to her anger was gone.

"I know," Matt answered. "And I had a lot of time to think about everything last night. I really am sorry. I didn't realize how big of a deal this really is. And I guess I have to admit I was a little jealous."

Carly cocked her head at her boyfriend. "Ya think?" she mocked.

Matt smiled sweetly. "Yes," he sighed. "So now that I've admitted that, maybe we can have breakfast, and bury the hatchet, so to speak."

Carly frowned at the unexpected cliché, but shrugged. The edge was definitely gone. She grabbed the flowers and set them inside the bedroom. "Okay, green-eyed monster," she teased. "Let's go have some bacon and eggs, and you can tell me how you slept on the couch."

As it turned out, there were no bacon and eggs, just some muffins and a note from the caretaker that she wouldn't be in that day.

"Must be because it's Sunday," Carly opined.

"Must be," Matt agreed. Then, as they each grabbed a muffin and sat down, he asked, "So, tell me about 'Pyromancer.'"

Carly's eyes widened a bit. Then she stared down intently

at her muffin. "Oh, it's nothing really. Just a silly thing I wrote along the way."

"What genre is it?" Matt asked. "Fantasy? Dystopian?"

Carly didn't look up. "Um, no. It's more, um, urban fantasy."

Matt nodded. "Oh, okay. Like vampires and werewolves?"

"Uh yeah, kind of," Carly finally met Matt's gaze and smiled. "It's set in the city, and there's this, uh, cop, who, uh, gets like fire powers. And um, he uses them to solve crimes and stuff."

Matt nodded, a sad smile unfolding across his face. "I read your query."

Carly's eyes flared again. "What?!"

"Last night, while you were sleeping. I read your query. You stole 'Ring of Fire.' You stole my book."

Carly set the muffin down and took a long, deep breath. "Okay, Matt. First of all, I did not steal your book. 'Ring of Fire' sucked. It was all over the place, made no sense, had plot holes and loose ends everywhere, and your protagonist was one-dimensional and unlikable at the same time."

This time it was Matt's eyes that flared, but he didn't say anything.

"I changed it completely," Carly went on. "Made the main character a woman, added some bad guys who were truly evil, and reset it on a dystopian world where the sun had gone out. You set yours on Hawaii. Who cares about fire powers when it's eighty degrees and sunny every day?"

"You could have helped me fix it, Carly," Matt growled. "But you stole it. That was my story. My idea. That should have been my full request. My R and R."

"Don't flatter yourself, Matt," Carly sneered. "You did

everything you could with that manuscript but it was the same crap you always write. I took that kernel of an idea and turned it into a real novel."

She stood up and dropped her paper napkin on the table. "In fact, I'm going to go see if Eva fucking Margolis is my agent yet. And then I'm calling a cab."

Matt watched her strut out of the dining room. He waited a moment, then followed after her. He wasn't sure what he was going to say or do but he wasn't just going to sit there and take it.

He climbed the stairs forcefully, his hand squeezing the banister harder with each stomp up the steps. When he reached the top, his blood was boiling.

Then she appeared.

The woman from his dreams. Helen Montchartes.

"It's your story," Helen's ghost echoed in his ear. "Take it back."

"How?" Matt practically pleaded. "She's the one who changed it. She's the one who got the full request."

"Tell Margolis you did all that. Tell her it's your story. Claim your fate."

Matt looked down, unsure.

"Do it for me," Helen whispered. "My fate was stolen from me too by publishers who didn't understand me. I understand, Matthew. I understand you. Do it for me."

Matt looked up, wild eyed. But he shook his head. "She'll tell."

Helen's wraithlike body glowed brighter. "Make it so she can't tell."

Matt didn't have time to process the thought before Carly came running out of the bedroom, dispersing Helen's form into the air.

"She accepted it! Eva fucking Margolis accepted my manuscript! I'm agented!"

Matt's eyes flared with rage. "No, you're not." He grabbed her by the shoulders. "I am."

And he threw her down the stairs.

Carly had no chance to grab the banister or otherwise break her fall. She bounced off the wooden steps and landed in a heap at the bottom, her neck broken, dead eyes staring up from her grotesquely angled head.

Helen reappeared at Matt's side. "You did that for me."

Matt didn't answer. His heart and mind were racing beyond capacity for thought. He thought his next step would be emailing Eva fucking Margolis, then taking the body out to the woods to bury it.

Helen could read his thoughts. "No, Matthew. You can't leave the house now. You're mine. You're mine forever."

Matt turned to look at Helen. She was no longer the beautiful woman of her youth. She was a thinly covered skeleton, with empty eye sockets and exposed cheekbones.

"I— I didn't mean to—" Matt stammered.

"Mine," Helen Montchartes ghost repeated, and a ring of fire flamed up around the house. "Mine forever."

"No!"

But it wasn't Matt who shrieked the word. It was Carly. Her own ghost, rising up the stairs, head laying sickeningly on her shoulder. "He's mine!" Carly cackled. "Mine forever."

"Mine!" shrieked Helen.

"Mine!" screeched Carly.

Matt screamed too, but no one would ever hear him again.

MEET THE AUTHORS

Dawn Kirby lives in West TX with Jamie, her husband of 17 years and their three children. She's the author of the paranormal romance, *Secrets*, book one in the Serenity Series published by Twisted Core Press. Book two and three, *Deceit* and *Tribulations* is set to be released later this year. Her short, "Sinful Pleasures (Lust)" appears in the *Seven Deadly Sins* anthology published by 7DS BOOKS. "A Devil in Leather" appears in 7DS's *Seven Deathly Soles* anthology. "A Perfect Mess" appears in 7DS's *Seven Dress Sizes*. "Stoic" appears in *A Man's Promise*. In addition, another short, "Date Night" was published in *13 Tales of the Paranormal* from Firefly and Wisp Publishing.

Well into a mid-life career change, **Quincy J. Allen** been published in multiple anthologies, online and print magazines as well as one omnibus. His steampunk version of *Steampelstiltskin* is under contract with Fairy Punk Studios, and he's written for the Internet radio show *RadioSteam*. His novel *Chemical Burn*—a finalist in the Rocky Mountain Writers Association Colorado Gold Writing Contest—was first published in June of 2012. His new novel *Jake Lasater: Blood Curse*, is currently being shopped around, and he's started work on a new off-world steampunk series titled Paragon. He works part-time as a tech-writer to pay his bills, does book design and eBook conversions for Word Fire Press, and lives in a lovely house that he considers his very own sanctuary.

 **Chrissy Moon** calls both Los Angeles and Seattle home. In addition to writing novels such as *Surreal Ecstasy* and *DayDreamer*, Chrissy likes to spend her time being petrified of well-made horror movies while laughing hysterically at the many bad ones.

 **Julianne Snow** is the author of the *Days with the Undead* series. She writes within the realms of speculative fiction and has roots that go deep into horror. Julianne has pieces of short fiction in publications from Sirens Call Publications, Open Casket Press, James Ward Kirk Publishing, and Hazardous Press as well as the forthcoming shorts in anthologies from 7DS Books, Phrenic Press, and the Coffin Hop charity anthology *Death by Drive-In*. Look for parts in a number of collaborative projects to be announced shortly.

Kat Daughtry is a twisted Southern Belle from the Dirty South drawn to the romance, erotica, and steampunk side of the literary world. She has several short stories published and recently released her debut novel, *Steamfate*. She loves tattoos (in moderation). She hates television (except PBS and old movies). She believes in dream meanings, fate, aliens and love at first sight. To learn more about Kat, read her work or pay attention to tweets and facebook posts.

Jess Russell has been writing stories, blogs, poetry, and other shenanigans since early youth. She studied psychology in college. Her favorite genre is fantasy/Science Fiction. Jess is currently a stay at home mom, residing in Rochester, NY, with her son, fiancé and two cats.

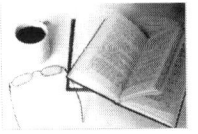

Michael Hillcrest is an author from the Great Pacific Northwest. He has written several short stories and collaborated on a novel. He is looking to commit to greater projects in the near future.

14264546R00104

Printed in Poland
by Amazon Fulfillment
Poland Sp. z o.o., Wrocław